THE MODERN ARK

SAVING ENDANGERED SPECIES

DANIEL COHEN

illustrated with photographs

G. P. Putnam's Sons   New York

Photograph credits

© Ron Austing, © Cincinnati zoo photograph, page 3.
Jessie Cohen, National Zoological Park, Smithsonian Institute, pages 61, 81.
Henry Poorly Zoo, Omaha, page 105.
Jim Driscoll, page 53.
Jack Grisham, OKC Zoological Park, page 92.
Los Angeles zoo, page 31.
Mel Woods, Point Defiance Zoo and Aquarium, pages 15, 21.
Wyoming Game and Fish Department, page 43.
© Zoological Society of San Diego 1992, photo by Ron Garrison, page 71.

G. P. Putnam's Sons, a division of The Putnam & Grosset Group,
200 Madison Avenue, New York, NY 10016.
G. P. Putnam's Sons, Reg. U.S. Pat & Tm. Off.
Published simultaneously in Canada
Printed in the United States of America
Book design by Patrick Collins. Text set in Aster

Library of Congress Cataloging-in-Publication Data
Cohen, Daniel, 1936   The modern ark / Daniel Cohen.   p.   cm.
Includes bibliographical references (p.).
1. Endangered species—Juvenile literature. 2. Wildlife conservation—Juvenile
literature. 3. Captive wild animals-Breeding—Juvenile literature. [1. Endangered
species—Breeding. 2. Wildlife conservation.] I. Title.
QL83.C64 1995   333.95′16—dc20   94-34007 CIP AC
ISBN 0-399-22442-4

10 9 8 7 6 5 4 3 2 1

First Impression

13992

To Rosie M.

CONTENTS

CHAPTER 1

THE MODERN ARK

AS OUR HUMAN SPECIES EXPANDS, the natural world shrinks. Almost every day we hear about pollution, poaching, and the destruction of habitats. Animal species that have existed for hundreds of thousands, even millions, of years are in danger of becoming extinct and disappearing forever.

Many other species, which include some of the best known and best loved animals in the world, have been so severely reduced in number that they may not survive much longer. These are the endangered species.

The news about the plight of endangered species sometimes is so relentless and so depressing that one feels overwhelmed and helpless. It is absolutely true that the problems facing endangered species in today's world are enormous. Yet heroic and often successful efforts are being made right now to save as many of these species as possible, in a worldwide program called "captive breeding"—breeding endangered animals in captivity to preserve the species, and hopefully returning them to the wild one day. A lot of this captive breeding is happening

1

in the most surprising, and unlikely, places, as I was to discover.

I watched the small herd of black rhinoceroses moving placidly about in the shadow of a huge roller coaster. I was behind the scenes at an amusement/wild animal park in Ohio, a place where the casual visitor is not allowed to go. In fact, the casual visitor would not even know the rhino herd existed.

It was early in the year, and the roller coaster wasn't operating yet.

"Doesn't the roller coaster bother them?" I asked.

"Oh, no," the man in charge replied. "The rhinoceros isn't a particularly sensitive animal. Once the roller coaster starts it takes the rhinos about a month to notice that anything is happening. And then they don't seem to mind."

One of the rhinos pressed itself up against the thick iron railing that surrounded the corral. "Scratch her behind the ear," the man in charge told me. "She likes that."

So I reached over and began to scratch behind the rhino's ear. The skin was remarkably soft at that spot, and I suspect that it is just about the only place on a rhino where scratching would be felt. And she did seem to enjoy it.

"They have a bad reputation," said the man in charge. "They are really very gentle."

What I did not notice was that one of the rhinos in the middle of the corral had noticed me, didn't like what it

2

The black rhinoceros

saw, and charged. It struck the metal fence in front of me with a resounding clang, and I swear it bent the two-inch-thick metal bar.

"Oh," the man in charge said, calmly, "that one tends to be a bit nervous with strangers."

Being charged by a rhinoceros in the middle of Ohio is truly a unique experience. The black rhino is a native of Africa, and there are only a few hundred of them left in their natural habitat. So what are all these severely endangered black rhinos doing at an amusement park in the middle of Ohio?

They are not there primarily for display. They are part of a countrywide, indeed a worldwide, effort involving hundreds of zoos, wild-animal parks, and many other facilities, to save the endangered species of the world. Breeding threatened species in captivity is part of a brave and often desperate attempt to keep them from going the way of the dodo and passenger pigeon.

In the wild all species of rhino are severely endangered. Poachers and the unrelenting pressure caused by a growing human population on the land rhinos once freely roamed have contributed to this crisis. This amusement park in Ohio, far from the black rhino's African home, is one of the places where biologists and other zoo professionals are attempting to hold on to a remnant of these ancient and magnificent creatures, in the hope that someday the rhinos can be returned to at least a semblance of life in the wild. The rhinos are supposed to be protected in their African homeland, but the poor and sometimes unstable governments of many African nations often don't have the resources to adequately protect the rhinos, no matter how much they may want to do so. A nation where people are struggling just to get enough to eat does not have the luxury of worrying a great deal about endangered species.

Protecting endangered species is not an entirely new role for zoos. The famous Bronx Zoo in New York City was primarily responsible for saving the buffalo, or American bison, from extinction. It is far from the places where the buffalo roamed and were slaughtered in such enormous numbers. Because of people's indiscriminate hunting practices, the American bison was about as rare by the end of the last century as the black rhino is today. It was an endangered species. The Bronx Zoo, which opened in 1899, began purchasing bison from whatever sources it could, and started breeding them. The bison bred so freely in the zoo that in just a few years, some of them were sent out to a newly established bison reserve in Oklahoma. In 1913 another herd of Bronx-bred bison was sent out to South Dakota. The reintroduced bison prospered and, within a few years, the zoo was able to reduce the size of its captive herd and essentially go out of the bison-breeding business. Today the bison remains protected in the wild, but it is no longer an endangered species.

Animals like the Père David's deer and Asian wild horse were preserved in private collections owned by wealthy individuals and rulers, after they had disappeared in the wild. Had it not been for these privately owned and maintained herds, both these species would be extinct today.

Until fairly recent times the zoo was not considered a place where wild animals were protected and preserved. Zoos were for people, not animals. Animals were captured and put on display for the entertainment and education of the public. To tell the truth, most early zoos were pretty awful, little more than prison camps for animals.

Over time, zoos changed. In the better zoos there were attempts to make the displays more humane: animals were given more space and a more natural setting. Many captive animals lived long, healthy lives, and developed great affection for their keepers.

Some animals were bred in zoos. Baby animals were always popular exhibits, and it was often cheaper to breed an animal than to buy one. But essentially zoos continued to be consumers of wild animals. When an animal died, they bought another wild-caught animal to replace it. Often they didn't look too closely at how the animals were captured—an entire family of gorillas might be shot so that a single baby gorilla could be caught and sold to a zoo. Wild animals were routinely shipped under horrifying conditions, and many died before they ever reached their destinations.

As a child I was an obsessive zoo visitor. Only later did I learn that there was a dark and dirty underside to all those happy afternoons I spent going to the monkey house or the lion house. It wasn't that zoo people were cruel—far from it. Most were absolutely devoted to the animals they cared for. But the general philosophy, not just in the zoo but almost everywhere, was that nature was inexhaustible; that there was an endless number of animals out there in the wild, and that taking a few for a zoo would not diminish the overall wild population.

In fact, the experiences with the bison, the passenger pigeon, and other species that once had been numerous and had been hunted to extinction or nearly so, showed quite clearly that nature is by no means inexhaustible. But the lesson was very slow to sink in, and by the time it did, the survival prospects were dim for many, many species.

By the 1970s the United States and other countries had

begun to restrict and ultimately ban the capture and importation of a large number of endangered species. It was not enough for a country such as India to outlaw the capture and exportation of tigers, because if there are buyers there will always be sellers. Countries like the United States, where zoos can afford to pay large sums for desirable animals, like tigers, also had to cooperate by agreeing not to buy them. A wide variety of international agreements was required. If they had continued in their old ways, many zoos simply would have gone out of business because they would have been unable to get the animals they needed for display. So breeding animals in zoos became a much more serious business. Today more than 90 percent of all mammals and 70 percent of all birds in North American zoos were born in captivity.

By the 1980s zoos had expanded their mission. Not only would they breed animals to populate their own exhibits, but they would also breed endangered species to keep them from becoming extinct, with the hope that some day animals could be returned to the wild from which they had disappeared, or where they had been so reduced in numbers that their survival was in serious doubt.

That is an ambitious program. A huge percentage of the world's animal species, thousands of them, face extinction by the end of this century. If you could gather together all the professionally run zoos and aquariums in the world, they would fit in an area of about seventy square miles, the size of the borough of Brooklyn, New

York. Obviously these institutions can aid in the survival of only a tiny percentage of the world's threatened species. The ultimate key to the survival of species is protection of the total environment, not breeding animals in zoos.

But to say that zoos can't do everything is not the same as saying they can do nothing. What they try to do now is embodied in what is called the Species Survival Plan, or SSP.

The SSP was created in the 1980s by zoo directors, curators, zoologists, and other professionals, like Ulysses Seal, William Conway, Dennis Meritt, Edward Schmitt, and Tom Foose. At one time zoos were fiercely independent institutions that often competed with one another. Yet no one zoo, no matter how large, can really be responsible for saving even a single species. If zoos are to fulfill their role of preserving endangered species, then they have to cooperate and share information, space, and animals. They have to surrender some of their independence for the greater good.

First a decision has to be made regarding which species will be part of the SSP. That decision is made by representatives from all the participating zoos. One of the most controversial aspects of the program is that the species chosen most often are "flagship species," well-known animals that arouse strong feelings in the public, such as the black rhinoceros, the cheetah, the giant panda, and the gorilla. The program also includes some lesser-known animals, like the Rodrigues' fruit bat, the Guam rail, the

8

Puerto Rican crested toad, some fish, and even a rare species of snail. But for the most part, the animals in the SSP are large, interesting mammals.

There is a species coordinator for every specific plan, each of which covers a single species. There is one plan for the black rhino, one for the cheetah, and so on. The coordinator is aided by a variety of experts, from zoologists to zookeepers, who know about the particular animal. Animals are bred in specific zoos. For example, a zoo in Nebraska may not be able to get a clouded leopard for exhibit, even though it wants one and has room for one, because clouded leopards are being bred elsewhere. Under the SSP no single zoo really owns any endangered animal. The animals may be shifted from zoo to zoo on breeding loan when they are needed. If an animal is infertile or is past breeding age, it may be sent to some other zoo for exhibit only, so as to make room for an animal that can breed. A gorilla may be owned by the Cleveland zoo, for example, and may have been on display there for many years. But if those who run the SSP for the gorilla decide the breeding potential for this gorilla would be greater somewhere else, off it goes. Regular zoogoers are sometimes puzzled and angered when a popular animal, one that they have been watching for years and have come to love, is suddenly sent away. The dangers facing so many animal species are grave. There is little time or room for sentiment.

At one time it was the aim of most zoos to display examples of as many different species as possible. The aim of the modern zoo is to keep a larger number of individual animals from a smaller number of species, and keep them in conditions that more closely resemble the world in which their ancestors lived. A pair of gorillas, or even a single gorilla, would have been enough for the average-sized zoo. But if the aim is to breed gorillas, just having one gorilla, or even a pair, isn't going to do much good. Gorillas live and breed best in large family groups. Not all zoos have the facilities to properly house eight or ten gorillas. So the gorillas of breeding age are kept mainly in those zoos where they can be bred most effectively.

On the other hand, African lions breed very well in captivity, under practically any circumstances. The African lion is not an endangered species, and some zoos don't want to use their limited space for lions. The last time I went to the Bronx Zoo, I couldn't even find a lion on display. Though there must have been a lion or two somewhere, they are nowhere near as prominent as they once were. The space is needed for more-threatened species.

Inbreeding among small captive populations of zoo animals can create serious genetic problems. One of the main responsibilities of the SSP is keeping track of the genetic history of all the animals of the species that are part of the plan. It is much like keeping the pedigree of purebred dogs or racehorses. On the basis of this information, the species coordinator can make recommendations about which animal should go where, and who should be bred with whom.

10

Genetic information about captive animals throughout the world is kept at the International Species Information System (ISIS) at the zoo in Apple Valley, Minnesota. This information is stored in one large computer database. By consulting the computer, one can find out about the family history of a zebra in Switzerland or a tree kangaroo in Seattle.

More than conventional zoos are involved in the program. Some large institutions, like the National Zoo in Washington, D.C., and the Bronx Zoo in New York, have special off-site breeding facilities in Fort Royal, Virginia, and on St. Catherine's Island, Georgia, respectively. These are facilities for animals only. Visitors are not allowed. Several other large zoos are planning to open similar special breeding centers.

Such places as the San Diego Wild Animal Park, and the Fossil Rim Wildlife Center in Texas, have large areas that provide critically needed space for raising animals that live in herds. Private wildlife ranches and even amusement parks that have wildlife exhibits cooperate in the SSP. That's why there was a herd of black rhinos under the roller coaster in the middle of Ohio. It was one of the designated rhino breeding centers.

Whenever possible the SSPs try to include reintroduction projects—that is, put captive-bred animals back into the wild. For native American species these projects are often carried out in cooperation with various government agencies, like the U.S. Fish and Wildlife Service. While reintroduction is an admirable goal, all too often there is no wild left for an animal to be returned to. For the time

11

being at least, the last best hope for many severely endangered species may be the zoo.

There are a lot of critics of the SSP. The critics range from animal rights activists who don't think any animal should be kept in captivity for any reason, to environmentalists who say that too much time, effort, and money is spent on saving a few popular zoo animals, while the real problem is preserving the environment for all species. Those who are involved in the SSP acknowledge that there is a lot of truth in what the critics say. But they like to tell a story about Noah. The story goes that when Noah started building the ark, a lot of people thought he was foolish. They stood around and said that it wasn't needed, or it wouldn't work, or it couldn't be finished in time. Then the rain began to fall. But the critics still would not be silent.

Finally Noah turned to the critics and said, "Look, the water is already up to your knees. Either grab a hammer, or get out of the way."

The plan for each species is different: different problems, different solutions. In the chapters that follow, we will take a closer look at some of the best known modern attempts to save endangered species.

CHAPTER 2

THE RED WOLF DILEMMA

THERE ARE A LARGE NUMBER of laws and regulations protecting endangered species. But what about protecting an endangered *sub*species? or an endangered *race?* or an endangered *hybrid?* A question like that may sound like hairsplitting. But it's not. It is very serious. It has come up in the case of the red wolf, subject of one of the most ambitious and apparently successful of all the captive breeding and release programs ever attempted in the United States.

The animal we all think of when we hear the word "wolf" is the gray timber wolf, scientific name *Canis lupus,* that once roamed the forests of Europe, Asia, and North America. This is the Big Bad Wolf, pictured as a ferocious killer and relentless enemy of humanity in everything from the Bible to the folktales of the Brothers Grimm. The wolf inspired, and sometimes still inspires, a fear and hatred among people far in excess of any possible harm it could do.

But in North America there is another kind of wolf, the red wolf, *Canis rufus.* Despite the name, the red wolf isn't always red or even reddish. Some animals have a reddish cast to their coats, but the color varies from tawny to gray and occasionally black. The gray wolf isn't always gray either. The main difference between the red and gray wolf is size. A fully grown gray wolf may weigh one hundred pounds, but a red wolf rarely exceeds eighty. It is still larger than another near relative, the coyote, which is about forty pounds. The red wolf is also more elusive and solitary than the gray, which is a sociable pack hunter.

According to one theory the ancestors of all modern wolves appeared first in North America. Some stayed and became red wolves. Others wandered into Eurasia, where over the years they evolved into gray wolves. Then during the next to last Ice Age the grays came back, bigger, stronger, and more successful than the reds. Gradually they drove the red wolves out of the forests and into the inhospitable swamps and brambles of what is now the southeastern United States and Texas. There the red wolves hung on until a wave of human immigrants— European settlers—arrived with their guns, plows, axes, poison, and traps, and very nearly wiped them out.

The settlers were no better to the gray wolves, which were ruthlessly exterminated over the vast majority of their North American range, but gray wolves still survived in sufficient numbers in Canada and Alaska so as not to be threatened with extinction. The red wolves, which had never been that numerous, had no such refuge. They were being squeezed into an ever smaller and less hospitable territory.

14

The red wolf

For a long time people were interested only in getting rid of wolves because they were thought to be a threat to people and domestic animals. But no one seemed to realize or care just how successful the extermination effort had been with the red wolf. The problem was that this type of wolf was so reclusive, lived in such inhospitable places, and so closely resembled both the coyote and gray wolf that, until the 1960s, no one was really aware that the species was in serious trouble. By that time attitudes toward endangered species had started to change, but it was very nearly too late for the red wolf.

Not only was this severely threatened species not being protected, but in parts of Texas and Louisiana, the red wolf's last stronghold, bounties of ten to twenty dollars were still being offered for every dead wolf, as opposed to only one or two dollars for a coyote. An unemployed cowboy could make good money killing wolves.

An even more immediate problem was hybridization. The division of the animal and plant worlds into neat categories is a human construction. In nature things are more flexible. Some closely related species never, or rarely, interbreed successfully. Others interbreed freely. The domestic dog, a direct descendant of the wolf, will breed both with wolves and coyotes. And the wolf will also breed with coyotes.

As the number of red wolves declined, the coyote, which is much more adaptable and successful at fending off its human enemies and coping with a man-made environment, began to take over red wolf territory. With fewer and fewer potential mates to choose from, red wolves began mating with coyotes. The result was a wolf-coyote hybrid, an animal smaller than the wolf, but larger than the coyote, which could easily be mistaken for either one.

By the 1960s a few biologists recognized that the red wolf population was shrinking fast. In 1967 the species was finally given some limited protection. When the Endangered Species Act was passed by Congress in December 1973, the red wolf was right at the top of the list for priority treatment. The act gave the federal government broad powers to preserve any native species on the verge of extinction.

A small team of scientists began to investigate the red wolf more closely, and discovered to their horror that its continued existence was far more precarious than anyone had imagined. Areas that they had once believed were inhabited only by "pure" wolves were found to contain a large number of wolf-coyote hybrids. The wolves themselves were generally in terrible shape. In the humid and swampy climate, which was the red wolf's last refuge, parasites thrived. The wolves were infested with hookworms, heartworms, and horrendous cases of mange mites. Any of these infestations could be fatal, and usually were. While captive red wolves can easily live fifteen years, they rarely survived more than five in the wild. The mortality rate among puppies was enormous.

There was already a small number of captive red wolves in zoos, though the red wolf had never been a popular zoo animal. In 1973 the Point Defiance Zoo in Washington State was designated the official breeding center for red wolves. The captive-bred animals were supposed to be a safeguard against the extinction of the red wolf in the wild. But when scientists took a closer look at the captive animals, they found that only six of the eighteen animals in the breeding program could be classed as pure wolves. All the rest were hybrids. Six was far too small a number for a successful captive breeding program.

Any number of plans were advanced to preserve the wild red wolf, but by 1975 those who ran the Red Wolf Recovery Project had reluctantly come to the conclusion that there was no way to save the red wolf in its current habitat. They decided that the only thing that could be done to preserve the species was to trap all the wild red wolves possible and use them as the basis for a vigorous captive breeding program. Once a stable captive population had been established, red wolves could be released in areas where the climate was better and where there were no coyotes.

This was a bold and risky decision. While it was assumed that the wild red wolves would breed fairly well in captivity, as gray wolves do, no one was really sure, because so little was known about the behavior of the animal.

Curtis Carley, who led the recovery project in its early days, recalled, "We were concerned that we were going against the very intent of the Endangered Species Act, which was to save animals in the *wild*. We knew also that if the political climate of the country changed [turned against reintroducing wolves] we might not ever be able to reintroduce the species, no matter how many animals we had in captivity. It was a real gamble. We felt we might eventually be blamed for the extermination of the red wolf.''

But it was a gamble that had to be taken. By the summer of 1980, when the wolf capture program finally ended, some four hundred wild canines had been trapped. Only forty of them looked like pure wolves, and these were admitted to the breeding program. Appearances could not always be trusted, however. Closer study, which involved, among other things, x-raying the animals' skulls, revealed that a mere seventeen showed no trace of coyote heritage. If there were still wild red wolves out there, they would not survive for long. The future of the species rested entirely on this tiny number of captive animals.

To prevent an epidemic or natural disaster from wiping out an entire population, the captive wolves were divided up among a number of zoos and wildlife facilities. But Point Defiance remained the center for the breeding program. The red wolf is neither a spectacular nor a popular zoo exhibit. Before the wolf rescue program began, few zoos had ever exhibited one at all, but now at least a handful of institutions had built special quarters for them. Many of the captive wolves were not on display to the public.

Captive breeding programs rarely go smoothly, and the red wolf program was no exception. At Point Defiance newly captured wolves refused to breed at first. It took them well over a year to get used to captivity. Then there was an outbreak of parvo, a virus that was usually deadly to pups and which was also sweeping the domestic dog population. A vaccine was available, but before the virus was recognized a lot of wolf pups were lost.

By the mid 1980s the breeding program had really begun to work smoothly. There was a healthy and growing population of captive red wolves, about seventy-five in all. The aim had never been to provide the animals to zoos, but to return them to the wild. So those in charge of the captive breeding program began looking around for a place where the wolves could safely and successfully be released. Obviously they could not be put back into the same areas of Texas and Louisiana, where they would soon fall victim to the parasites and be overwhelmed by coyote hybrids, the same problems that had so very nearly caused their extinction a decade earlier.

The place chosen for the first release was the 141,000-acre Alligator River National Wildlife Refuge in North Carolina. There had been no wild wolves in that area for well over a century. Before the wolves were released, the U.S. Fish and Wildlife Service conducted an intensive public relations campaign in North Carolina to convince those who lived near the wildlife refuge that they had nothing to fear from their new neighbors. No one actually lived in the refuge itself, but it wasn't fenced, so it was

Animal care technician Sue Behrens holds the first-ever litter of red wolf pups conceived through artificial insemination.

probable that wolves would occasionally wander out. A hostile local population would be able to fuel political pressure to destroy the release program, or local hunters might simply kill the wolves. Luckily, although some people who lived near the refuge were suspicious of the release program, they were not overtly antagonistic.

Successfully releasing captive-born animals into the wild is far, far more difficult than most people imagine. It is not simply a matter of opening the cage door and waving good-bye. While in captivity every effort had been made to keep the wolves as "wild" as possible. They were raised in family groups, and contact with humans was kept to a bare minimum. But still, they lived in fenced enclosures, rather than ranging over many square miles every day. They didn't hunt, but ate the same kind of food domestic dogs eat. And unlike wild animals, they had no reason to avoid humans and all their works, as truly wild wolves might. Most animals are not born with a neat package of "instincts" that allow them to live successfully in the wild. They are born with *certain* equipment— teeth, acute sight and hearing, etc. And they have *certain* instincts. A domestic cat, for example, will tend to hunt smaller animals, even if the only food it has ever eaten comes out of a can. But to survive successfully, most animals have to learn a lot about life. A wolf might "hunt" by instinct. But it would have to learn how to hunt well enough to survive in the wild.

The wolves were not released at once. They were kept in large, fenced enclosures on the reserve so they could slowly adjust to the climate and new living conditions. They were weaned away from dog food. First, "road kill" was given to them. Then live prey was introduced into the enclosures.

Finally, after six months of anxious waiting and observation, the red wolf rescue team opened the gates to the enclosures and let the wolves roam freely. Well, not quite freely. The wolves were outfitted with collars containing transmitters so that their activities could be monitored. The collars also contained remote-controlled tranquilizer darts. In theory if the wolves wandered out of the reserve, they could be put to sleep and brought back. That sounded like a good idea, but unfortunately it didn't work. The collars, however, were quite large and noticeable and provided the quickest way to tell whether an animal was a wolf or a German shepherd. During the first months after the release of the wolves, there were always a couple of biologists on hand at Alligator River to monitor the animals and to help them out if they got into trouble. The "wild" to which the red wolves had been returned was not so very wild after all.

The newly released red wolves did not immediately slink off into the woods and adopt the secretive ways of their ancestors. Some refused to leave the familiar enclosure for weeks after the doors were opened. Others displayed a remarkable and potentially fatal lack of fear of humans and automobiles.

In her book *Meant to Be Wild*, Jan DeBlieu described the experiences of biologists Chris Lucash and George Paleudis while tracking some newly released wolves. They were driving down a road at night when their headlights picked up the shine from a pair of eyes right in front of them. It was one of the wolves, and he was running toward the truck. The animal was not afraid of the headlights or the noise of the truck. A second wolf followed closely behind. "It was the last thing the young biologists had expected; they had not the faintest idea what to do. The animals continued to trot between the vehicles, cautious, but more curious than afraid. Lucash muttered cynically that they looked like pet dogs."

Over the next two weeks similar reports poured in. Time and again people said that the wolves acted like lost dogs. It was only after people spotted the obvious tracking collars that they knew these animals were wolves.

Despite all the precautions that had been taken to keep them as wild as possible, the released animals just did not understand that trucks and cars could hurt them. And they had no fear of people. There was a $100,000 fine and possible jail sentence for anyone found harming a red wolf, but if the wolves kept showing themselves, it would be only a matter of time until someone shot one.

There was worse to come. The wolves began roaming outside of wildlife areas and into people's yards. No wolves were shot, but a couple of biologists trying to trap them very nearly were. Local residents didn't like to have armed strangers running through their property.

One of the released wolves was hit by a car. Others died of disease or starvation. But slowly and painfully some of the survivors began to adapt to life on their own, and they even began to breed.

More wolves were being acclimated for release in other sites in the South. It was hoped that the wild population of red wolves could be raised to about 220 and that there would be 300 in thirty captive breeding programs. The Red Wolf Recovery Project looked as if it was well on its way to becoming the most successful captive breeding and release program in the United States.

Then something quite unexpected happened. In 1989 the U.S. Fish and Wildlife Service had commissioned a detailed genetic study of the red wolf. In June 1992 geneticists Robert K. Wayne and Susan M. Jenks published the results of their research. To their surprise they could find no genetic difference between the red wolves that had been released as part of the wolf renewal program and the quite common coyote–gray wolf hybrid. "We simply didn't find any evidence of a unique red wolf genotype," said Wayne. "Maybe it's there and we just missed it; we're in the process of doing more tests. Right now, though, I can't say that there's any good supporting evidence that the red wolf is a species."

Writing in the *New York Times Magazine,* Jan DeBlieu said that if the findings are confirmed, "it means that the federal government may have spent twenty years and hundreds of thousands of dollars to preserve a wild mutt."

Many scientists simply refuse to accept the Wayne-Jenks findings. They say that the type of genetic testing they used is too new to be reliable, and that the method has been wrong in the past. They say the geneticists were too narrow-minded and ignored obvious differences in appearance and behavior between the red wolves and the hybrids.

There are other possibilities. The red wolf may not be a full species, but a subspecies, or race, of the gray wolf, and that is why its genetic makeup is not unique. Wayne has suggested that the red wolf once may have been a unique species that was so badly reduced by trapping, poisoning, and habitat destruction that before the wolf recovery program began, the few survivors had already interbred with coyotes. "You could make a case that as the last living examples of an extinct species, these hybrids are worth saving," he said. "They're all we have left of a species that humans killed off."

Other scientists have pointed out that hybrid subspecies occur frequently in nature, and that their appearance is part of the evolutionary process. Even if what we call the red wolf is a hybrid, that does not mean it is in any way inferior or unnatural. And it doesn't mean that they should not be protected when they are endangered.

Unfortunately the Endangered Species Act, which is used to protect animals like the red wolf, extends protection only to pure species. Hybrids or subspecies are out of luck. Already opponents of the wolf recovery program have moved to block further red wolf releases on the grounds that it is not a pure species. The Red Wolf Recovery Project, which was not so long ago hailed as one of the great successes of captive breeding, has not been abandoned but it has been cut back.

It's not that so many people really object to the red wolf, or to the relatively small amount of money that has been spent to protect it, but rather that a lot of business and commercial interests have never liked the Endangered Species Act. They have always wanted to get rid of it. If a species is to be protected, then its habitat can't be changed or developed. Trees can't be cut down, and houses can't be built. The fewer the number of animals protected, the fewer obstacles there will be to commercial development. Similar objections about the genetic purity of a species have been raised about protection for the endangered Florida panther, the spotted owl of the Pacific Northwest, and other animals. Many environmentalists fear that these new genetic testing methods will be used to dramatically reduce the number of species that are now protected by law, by claiming many of them are not real or pure species.

A lot of biologists believe that scientific techniques have gotten way ahead of public policy. For example, if it turns out that hybrids are more common than previously believed and have unique characteristics, then perhaps the policy of not protecting hybrids and subspecies should be changed. Environmentalists expect a new fight over the Endangered Species Act.

The red wolf was on the leading edge of the captive breeding and recovery programs. Now it appears that the animal's fate may rest on new definitions of what types of animals will be granted our protection.

CHAPTER 3

THE INTERRUPTED FLIGHT OF THE CONDOR

IF THE CALIFORNIA CONDOR ever soars freely over the mountains of southern California again, it will mark the happy ending to the most emotionally charged episode in the attempt to preserve endangered species in America. But that happy ending can't be written yet.

The last wild condor in America was trapped on Easter Sunday, 1987. He became part of a frantic effort to save the species from extinction through captive breeding. Capturing wild condors was a drastic move, and one that was bitterly opposed by many who were devoted to saving the bird.

At first it appeared as if the critics would be proved wrong. The condors adapted well to captivity and began to breed prolifically. By early 1992 there were enough captive-born condors for those in charge of condor recovery to attempt reintroducing the birds into their former habitat. That was way ahead of schedule.

The reintroduction did not go well. Usually the problems in programs of this type are known only to the small number of people who are actually involved. The California condor, however, had attained celebrity status and the problems were right there on the evening news. There were pictures of newly released condors blundering into cliffs. If a condor was found dead or injured, it was a major story. The people running the reintroduction program decided that since the total number of California condors in the entire world was still so small, it would not be a good idea to expose too many of them to the risks of premature freedom. So early in 1994 some of the released birds were recaptured, and returned to the zoos in which they had been born.

A California conservation official assured reporters that this recapture did not mean the end of the condor reintroduction program, but that it was only a "bump" in the road.

The California condor has been on a very bumpy road for a long time.

The California condor is an unlikely star. Though it has become a symbol for wildness and freedom, it is in reality just a big vulture—a very big vulture. With its ten-foot wingspan, it is far and away the largest bird in North America. Soaring effortlessly, apparently without moving even a feather, the condor looks magnificent. On the ground, tearing at a rotting carcass, it is, to our eyes, grotesque. Yet while vultures generally have a poor reputation, the California condor has become a legend.

The ancestors of the bird that we call the California condor may once have ranged widely over much of North America, feeding on the carcasses of the many large animals that populated the continent. When the majority of these big mammals became extinct some 10,000 years ago, the subsequent reduction in available food may have contributed to the condors' migration to the coast and mountains of the West, where they could scavenge on the remains of sea mammals, elk, and antelope.

Some Native American tribes regarded the huge bird as nearly sacred. Others held it in low regard because it is a scavenger. But the condor was in no danger from the American Indians. European settlers, with their guns and poison, were another matter. In the nineteenth century the condor was trapped and shot for sport. Its avocado-size blue or green eggs were collected as curiosities. Even more damage was done by ranchers who put out poisoned carcasses, hoping to kill wolves and bears. The condors also were attracted to the carcasses, ate the poison, and died off in large numbers.

By the 1930s the condor was known to exist only in some of the mountain regions of southern California. Laws were passed to protect the birds. While the laws curbed some of the worst abuses, the condor population continued to fall. By the 1950s it was estimated that there were only about sixty California condors left. The total number didn't seem to be declining any further, but it certainly wasn't growing either. No one could feel secure about the continued existence of a bird species with such a tiny population.

The California condor breeds very slowly. The birds take six years to reach sexual maturity. Then typically, a

The condor

condor pair will lay only a single egg every second year. It takes a long time for a population like this to rebound. Every single bird is vital to the survival of the species.

The condor was acquiring an almost mythic reputation among some conservationists. It also got the reputation, undeserved as it turned out, as a creature that was so sensitive it could not survive in captivity. In the 1950s, when ornithologists from the San Diego Zoo wanted to capture a pair of condors to begin a captive breeding program, many of the conservation groups strongly opposed the plan, and as a result no permits for capturing condors were issued.

Years later, when the already small condor population went into a steep and nearly irreversible decline, some scientists looked back ruefully at that decision not to start a captive breeding program back in the 1950s. It would have been much easier, cheaper, and far less risky to have a captive breeding and reintroduction program while there still was a stable wild population.

Some fairly large tracts of land were set aside as condor reservations, but still the population of the birds did not recover. The pesticide DDT was a problem for the condors, as it was for so many birds. Occasionally a condor was shot; that was strictly illegal, but difficult to prevent. Lead poisoning was a more serious problem. While searching for food the condors would regularly come across piles of deer entrails left by hunters who had shot and then gutted their kill. The condor would then ingest fragments of the bullets, or buckshot, which are made of lead, and soon die.

Some conservationists opposed not only capturing any condors for captive breeding, but even fitting condors with tiny radio transmitters so they could be more carefully monitored or allowing observers to watch them closely. All this, they said, would be too intrusive and would disrupt the condor's life. But in South America, where the closely related Andean condor also was endangered, the birds were being successfully bred in captivity, and wild birds were fitted with transmitters and watched constantly without any apparent ill effects. The California condor's closest relative was not as fragile and reclusive as some had assumed.

By the 1980s the situation for the California condor had become so precarious that a number of highly controversial moves were made. Some condors were captured, fitted with radio transmitters, and released. They did not seem bothered by the device. A couple of condors were captured and kept in the zoo, not for display but for breeding purposes. A few condor eggs were taken from nests in the wild to be hatched in the zoo. The hope was that the condors would "double clutch," that is, when they found the egg missing they would lay a second egg the same season. Many species will do this, and so, it turned out, would the California condor.

At first hatching condor eggs in an incubator was difficult. The chicks had trouble escaping from the shell, and they had to be rescued by keepers with tweezers. Eventually the source of the trouble was discovered. The shells were stiffening and sticking to the chicks. The problem was solved by raising the humidity during hatching.

A more serious problem for raising captive-bred condors, indeed for raising many birds, is imprinting. While a bird is very young it will bond to whatever living thing happens to be feeding it. This bond is imprinted on the bird's behavior and will last throughout its lifetime. In the wild a condor will imprint on its parents, other condors. In a zoo it is likely to imprint on a zookeeper. A male condor that has bonded to human beings may develop normally, in a physical sense, but when he reaches maturity, he shows no interest in female condors but considerable interest in his keepers. To prevent this those involved in the condor breeding stayed out of sight behind one-way mirrors and fed the newly hatched condor chicks with hand puppets that looked like condors. Every move of the condor hatchlings was monitored on closed-circuit television. No other bird in history has had the benefit of so much technology and human ingenuity.

As a result the condor population in captivity began to increase. In the wild the condor population was rapidly declining. All the surviving condors were being closely monitored. By 1983 biologists were putting out the carcasses of calves in areas where the big birds lived, in an effort to keep them from feeding on contaminated carrion. But it wasn't working very well, and condors were still dying, mostly from lead poisoning. While hunting was banned within the actual condor reserve area, the birds ranged very widely in search of food. A ban on hunting in all areas frequented by condors was considered, but even if this had been possible, most conservationists figured that angry hunters would then shoot condors in revenge, thus making the situation even worse. While there is widespread support in the United States for preserving endangered species, the support drops off sharply among those who are in any way inconvenienced by the effort. Sabotage of conservation efforts, and just plain vandalism, are all too common.

Between November 1984 and April 1985, nine of the fifteen remaining wild condors either died or vanished and were presumed dead. It was the worst period for the California condor since the recovery program began. At that point the Condor Recovery Team, a scientific body charged with preserving the condor, recommended to the U.S. Fish and Wildlife Service that the remaining birds be trapped and taken to the San Diego Wild Animal Park and the Los Angeles zoo, to join the other condors already in the safety of captivity.

This was a difficult and emotional decision. It was an admission that after years of trying and millions of dollars spent, it still had been impossible to save the wild condor. There were practical considerations as well. As long as wild condors remained in the mountain regions, a number of development projects had been blocked. As soon as the condors were gone there might be no limit to development within the condor's historic range. The National Audubon Society filed a suit against the U.S. Fish and Wildlife Service, seeking to block the capture of the last wild birds. After a court fight the Audubon Society lost. But in the end there really didn't seem to be much of a choice. It was either capture the condors, or watch the last few wild condors die, probably within a very few years.

The last free condor, a seven-year-old male dubbed AC-9, or Adult Condor 9, was captured in the Bitter Creek National Wildlife Refuge on Easter Sunday, 1987. Members of the Condor Recovery Team had been chasing him for nearly a year. Though this particular bird was quite used to the presence of human beings, he turned out to be remarkably difficult to catch. But that day he landed on a carcass that had been set out for him. Within minutes hidden cannons exploded, sending a mesh net cascading over the bird. His capture brought to an end the natural history of a species that had endured in North America at least since the Ice Age. If AC-9 and others of his kind were to survive, they would have to depend entirely on the dedication and skill of humans.

As soon as AC-9 was disentangled from the net, he was sent to the San Diego Zoo for two weeks of quarantine. Later he was taken to the San Diego Wild Animal Park. He joined twenty-six other captive condors. Their population was split between San Diego and Los Angeles.

The whole condor recovery project led to a lot of soul-searching among biologists and conservationists. There were those who had always opposed any sort of captive breeding program. They felt that in the end it was better simply to let an animal become extinct rather than turn it into a captive zoo exhibit. That was an extreme view.

A more serious criticism was that all the time, effort,

and money—some $25 million—that had been lavished on the effort to save this one species was simply out of proportion with its biological value. The California condor is held up as a prime example of what are called "charismatic megafauna," a small number of threatened species that are cute enough or distinctive enough to capture public imagination and public funds. Faith Campbell of the Natural Resources Defense Council has said, "Of 676 native species on the endangered or threatened lists, only around two dozen are receiving a significant amount of recovery effort." Defenders of the program reply that efforts like the condor recovery program focus public attention on the plight of threatened species in general. The condor serves as a flagship for many other species. Besides, if the money were not spent on the condor, there is absolutely no guarantee that it would go to save threatened snails or endangered wildflowers.

The ultimate success of this high-profile program would be measured not merely in the ability of biologists to get condors to breed in captivity—but to return them to nature. After AC-9 was captured, some in the program talked hopefully of beginning to return condors to the wild by the end of the century. That turned out to be a very conservative guess, for they had reckoned without the success of captive breeding.

In the wild condor eggs had about a 50 percent hatch rate. In captivity the hatch rate was more than 90 percent. There were fears that since the condor population had been so tiny, it would be terribly inbred. Genetic studies showed that the captive condor population was indeed inbred, but that didn't seem to affect them. The birds being born in captivity were extremely healthy. "Pretty soon we're going to be drowning in California condors," one researcher quipped.

By 1989, a mere two years after the last wild condor had been trapped, serious thought was being given to putting the condors back. But how was it to be done? Which techniques would work best? Despite the success of the breeding program, there were still fewer than seventy living California condors, and nobody was willing to experiment with them. So it was decided first to try to release the Andean condors, the larger South American relative of the California condor. If the release program was successful with the South American condor, it would probably succeed with the California variety. The Andean condor is also a threatened species, but not nearly so much at risk as the California condor. And there were plenty of captive-born Andean condors in zoos. Those to be released were hatched at the San Diego Wild Animal Park. There was no thought of permanently introducing the "alien" Andean condor to California. All of the birds released were female, to guard against any unplanned breeding. No one wanted to see the South American bird become established in California. All were fitted with radio transmitters and were to be recaptured and later turned loose in the home of their Andean forbearers.

The fledgling Andean condors had some difficulty adjusting to life in the California mountains, but they did well enough to encourage the condor recovery team to go on to the next, and most important, phase of their program—reintroducing the California condor itself.

In October 1991 two young captive-born California condors—Xewe, a female, and Chocuyens, a male—were taken to an enclosure on a rocky ledge in the Los Padres National Forest. This was the first step in acclimating them to living freely. They were accompanied by two Andean condors, to keep them company. In nature condors are gregarious. Both the young birds already wore tiny radio transmitters so that they could be tracked constantly.

On January 14, 1992, the pair were released into the wild. It was supposed to be an historic day. The young condors had a rough time at first because the Santa Ana winds were blowing fiercely, making it difficult for them to attain the soaring flight that is so characteristic of the condor. It took them about two months to really master flight. There were other problems. At one point during the summer, hunters shot at Xewe, but she escaped unhurt. By October all seemed to be going well. Then, on October 8, Chocuyens was found dead on a cliff in the northern part of Los Angeles County. The cause of death was unknown.

This death, after what appeared to be a successful start to the reintroduction program, was both a shock and a setback. But it did not bar future releases. However in 1993 more released condors died, and by 1994 some of the survivors were being recaptured and the release program was severely scaled back.

Unless there is a disaster, it is highly doubtful that the

release program will be abandoned entirely. There has been too much time, money, and prestige invested in it.

Even if the program ultimately succeeds, the California condor will not truly be returned to the wild. For the foreseeable future the condors' diet will have to be supplemented by "clean" carcasses set out by the condors' human watchers and protectors, in order to keep the birds from feeding off poisoned or lead-filled remains. They will have to be guarded from hunters who may try to shoot them, and from anyone who might try to disturb their vulnerable nests. Attempts will be made to "train" the condors to abandon their old free-flying ways, and confine themselves to an area where they will be relatively safe.

This bothers many conservationists. Jesse Grantham of the National Audubon Society said, "We're going to have a zoo species in the wild. That's all. Is *that* endangered species recovery? To me there's something missing. Was the intent of the Endangered Species Act to save animals by changing them to fit a man-altered habitat? I think that's a dangerous premise."

But the inescapable fact is that the California condor's habitat *is* man-altered. There is no way that the last hundred years of human history in California can be turned back. The best we can hope for is that the California condor can become a successful semiwild species. Otherwise the only California condor anyone is ever likely to see will be in the zoo.

CHAPTER 4

Back from the Brink

THE BLACK-FOOTED FERRET, or BFF, is such an elusive little creature that for a long time people didn't even know it existed. By the time people did realize there was such an animal, it seemed well on its way to extinction. In fact the species has been officially declared dead—twice. And twice it has come back from oblivion. The recent history of the BFF is like one of those old movie serials where at the end of each chapter, the hero or heroine appears to be utterly doomed. Yet when the next chapter begins he or she somehow manages to escape, only to face an even greater peril by the end of the episode.

The BFF is a weasel-like animal with light, buffy-yellow fur, a white belly, a black mask, and black legs. It's a smaller relative of the European species of ferret, which has been domesticated. The BFF is nocturnal, shy, and, at least for the last century or so, quite rare.

The creature was first described by John James Audubon in 1849. It preys exclusively on prairie dogs, and at that time billions of these rodents lived in burrows, often interconnected in vast complexes called "towns," on the

Great Plains. The prairie dogs, which are grass eaters, competed with cattle for food, and a cow or horse could break a leg by stepping into a prairie-dog hole. They were therefore considered a nuisance, and at the beginning of the twentieth century there was a determined and largely successful effort to wipe them out. Prairie dogs were shot, dynamited, and poisoned by government order. By the 1970s the prairie dog population had been reduced by more than 90 percent, and the black-footed ferret, which depended on prairie dogs for its food, had been very nearly eliminated as a result.

From the mid-1940s to the mid-1950s only a relative handful of the ferrets were found, and by 1960 the United States government was seriously considering whether to declare them extinct. Then in 1964 a small population was located in southwest South Dakota. The South Dakota ferrets were carefully studied, and biologists came to the conclusion that the population was too small and too scattered to provide much hope of long-term survival. By 1971 a few of the remaining BFFs were captured, in the hope that they would form the nucleus of a captive breeding program.

The greatest danger to the captive population was disease. BFFs were known to be susceptible to distemper, a disease common to domestic dogs. There is a vaccine for distemper, which has been effective for Siberian polecats, the species' closest relative. The captive ferrets were inoculated, but instead of protecting them the vaccine gave them distemper and they all died.

Black-footed ferrets

A few more ferrets were trapped but they died without producing any offspring. After 1974 no more of the animals were seen in South Dakota, and once again it appeared as if the little black-footed ferret had become extinct. That view prevailed until September 1981, when a dog belonging to a Wyoming ranch family killed one that had ventured into the yard.

Almost immediately a variety of biologists, conservationists, and others interested in endangered species descended upon the village of Meeteetse, Wyoming. The first estimate, made in 1982, was that there were about 60

43

ferrets living in the area. It was known, however, that the ferret population could fluctuate a good deal from year to year. In the late summer of 1984 there were an estimated 128 ferrets. Their range was limited, and the population was still so small that no one felt very comfortable about the prospects for their ultimate survival.

Almost from the start there was a conflict over whether a captive breeding program should be started. Some, mostly professional biologists and those who had zoo connections, advocated trapping a few of the animals immediately, before an epidemic or some other natural catastrophe could destroy them. Local fish and game officials, who had considerable influence over what was to be done, had a very different outlook. They generally resented outsiders coming in and telling them what to do. And they were deeply suspicious of captive breeding and reintroduction programs, which they felt had not been notably successful in the past. They too wished to preserve the BFF, but they believed the best way to do it was to leave them alone as much as possible. Local officials didn't even like the idea of putting radio collars on ferrets so that they could be tracked effectively.

There were also money problems. The political climate was not favorable to spending large sums of money on the preservation of obscure species. The Secretary of the Interior, James Watt, believed in turning as much as possible over to local control. But if there was to be local control, that also meant that the local people had to pay for whatever was done. Some captive breeding programs could be expensive, and Wyoming didn't have much of a budget for endangered species preservation.

It wasn't until 1985 that a plan to capture a limited number of ferrets was agreed upon, and then it was very nearly too late. The local prairie dog population had been infected with sylvatic plague, a disease spread by fleas. The plague did not appear to affect the ferrets directly, but it was rapidly killing off their only source of food. Field studies showed that the BFF population was diminishing.

Local authorities tried to control the spread of the disease by dusting prairie dog burrows with a pesticide to kill the fleas. Some of the professionals complained that the job was being done badly. At this moment of crisis there was very nearly open warfare among the various factions that were trying to save the black-footed ferret from imminent extinction. No one could agree upon a plan.

In the fall of 1985, six ferrets were finally captured and then housed in a state research station. Within two months they were all dead from distemper. The animals had probably picked up the disease naturally from other wild animals such as badgers, skunks, or coyotes. However, there was a suspicion that the virus had been brought in on the clothing of researchers or those who were applying the pesticide. Hostility ran deep.

There was nothing to be done but try to capture more ferrets before they disappeared entirely, and handle them even more carefully. A new isolated breeding facility was built in Sybille Canyon, some forty-five miles north of

Laramie, Wyoming. Decontamination procedures at the center were elaborate. Before entering the room in which the ferrets were kept, a visitor had to shower, put on special sterilized coveralls, and wear a surgical mask. No one was taking any unnecessary chances of spreading disease among the tiny number of captive ferrets.

A second building held a colony of Siberian polecats. These are closely related to the BFF, but they are also relatively common and breed well in captivity. The black-footed ferret, on the other hand, had never been successfully bred in captivity. It was hoped the polecats would provide clues to ferret mating behavior. For a while it looked as if the ferrets never would breed. The newly captured animals were badly unsettled, and the females chased away the males. Then in February 1987, researchers trapped what might have been the last Meeteetse ferret. He was a mature male, and from the evidence of healed wounds on his muzzle, this animal had been in some fights, perhaps with predators or with other ferrets. He was dubbed Scarface.

Scarface had not forgotten the mating rituals learned in the wild. A female was brought to his cage, which was equipped with a camera. The scientists watched on video screens to see what happened. There was a brief but fairly ferocious fight, and then, according to one of the researchers, "he just plain overpowered her." He later did the same with other females.

In 1987 seven kits, as the ferret's young are called, were born and weaned at the Sybille center. They were the first captive-born BFFs ever to survive. After that it

46

seemed as if the dam broke. Suddenly the little animals began breeding prolifically. Scarface produced so many descendants that he had to be retired, out of fear that his genes would be overrepresented in the species. Actually he wasn't fully retired; he was bred to Siberian polecats. This has produced some interesting hybrid offspring.

Within a few years the black-footed ferret captive breeding program was recognized as one of the most astonishingly successful in history. At the end of the 1990 season, there were 180 captive BFFs at Sybille Canyon, ten times the number there had been just a few years earlier. The recovery team was able to do something that they had wanted to do for a long time: split up the captive population so that a single catastrophe would not threaten the entire species. There was no proof that any BFFs still survived in the wild. None has been definitely identified since Scarface was trapped in 1987. But there are rumors of sightings and, given this animal's history, it is not inconceivable that that there may still be a few out there somewhere.

Some of the captive-bred ferrets were sent to the National Zoo's research facility at Fort Royal, Virginia. Others went to the Omaha Henry Doorly Zoo. Later zoos in Colorado Springs, Louisville, Toronto, and Phoenix also received a group of the little animals. You may not be able to see any on display yet, but if they continue to breed as prolifically as they have, some will undoubtedly be used for that purpose. Like their European and Asian relatives, these ferrets have adapted well to captivity.

However, the purpose of the captive breeding program

has not been just to produce another zoo animal. The hope has always been that the black-footed ferret would be returned to the wild. A major worry was whether captive-born animals had lost the skills that are required to survive in the wild. Tests showed that young BFFs had lost none of their skills for hunting and catching prairie dogs. But when it came to protecting themselves, that was another matter. In nature, badgers, owls, and other larger animals prey upon the ferrets. The captive-born BFFs didn't seem to react quickly enough to the presence of such danger. Some of the ferrets were trained through exposure to a stuffed owl suspended from a fishing line. The owl could menace the young ferrets, but not actually hurt them. They were also chased by RoboBadger, a stuffed badger mounted on the chassis of a Radio Shack remote-controlled toy truck. Whether this sort of training will be good enough is something that only time can tell.

Another, and potentially even more serious, problem is that the prairie dog population has been so drastically reduced that there are only a handful of places left in the country where a stable population of black-footed ferrets could be reintroduced and not starve. Two hundred ferrets would need as many as 25,000 acres of grasslands colonized by prairie dogs. Yet federal biologists were having trouble finding prairie dog towns as large as 1,000 acres. Back around the turn of the century, there was one prairie dog town in Texas that was 100 miles long and 250 miles wide.

But since the black-footed ferret breeds so well in captivity, there will probably be several attempts to reestablish it in the wild. Even if the first ferrets starve or are killed, those in charge of the project will undoubtedly find ways of protecting and providing food for animals released later. The ferrets will be slowly weaned from human aid as they learn to live on their own.

After several close brushes with total extinction, the future of the little ferret looks a lot brighter than it has for a very long time.

CHAPTER 5

THE TRAVELER

NOT FAR FROM WHERE I LIVE is the hawk watch platform at Cape May Point, New Jersey. Each autumn tens of thousands of hawks fly over the platform on their southward migration. It is, arguably, the finest place to see hawks in North America.

On a good day, when a cold front has passed and there is a northwest wind blowing, a couple of hundred people, armed with binoculars and 'scopes, may gather on the platform and spill over into the adjacent parking lot to see the migrating hawks pass overhead.

The premier birder today is not the proverbial little old lady; it is a young man, probably in his twenties, with the physique of an athlete and the eyes of—well, a hawk. These guys are truly amazing. They can determine the species, sex, and sometimes even the age of a passing hawk, with the naked eye, while with my binoculars all I can make out is a distant spot moving across the sky.

These experts don't usually bother to call out the more common hawks, like the broad-winged and red-tailed, which pass over by the thousands during September,

October, and November. But they will shout out every time they see one of the less common hawks. And there is one cry that brings everybody's binoculars swiveling toward a point in the sky—"Peregrine!"

The peregrine falcon is a *Guinness Book of World Records* sort of bird. The name means "traveler," and the peregrine is the most widespread bird in the world. It is native to every continent except Antarctica. It is also the fastest bird in the world. While pursuing its prey in a dive, the peregrine can reach speeds estimated at up to 200 miles per hour. A peregrine can spot potential prey at a distance of 3,000 feet. It is, all in all, a remarkable bird.

The peregrine falcon was never really numerous in North America. But, unlike many other birds, it did not seem to have suffered greatly from human interference. Evidence indicates that the number of peregrines did not decline perceptibly from the time the first Europeans began to settle the North American continent until the 1940s, despite the enormous changes in the environment that had taken place.

By the 1960s, however, the populations of many bird species had fallen dramatically, and one of the birds most severely affected was the peregrine falcon. The peregrine had disappeared east of the Mississippi, and the Western population was declining rapidly. It looked as if the peregrine falcon was on its way to extinction in the continental United States, and possibly throughout the world. At first no one knew what was happening to this tough and adaptable bird.

51

The villain was ultimately discovered, though the discovery took a long time. It turned out to be a group of pesticides, particularly the popular DDT. In the years following World War II, DDT was hailed as a wonder bug-killer, a substance that would rid us of everything from potato bugs to mosquitoes. What few realized at first was that the substance poisoned not only bugs, but also the birds and animals that ate the bugs, and its effects were felt right up the food chain. The devastating effects of DDT were detailed in Rachel Carson's epic-making book *Silent Spring*, published in 1962.

The impact of DDT on peregrine falcons and other birds of prey was not a direct one, and that is why it was difficult to recognize at first. The birds of prey would eat animals whose bodies contained small concentrations of pesticide residue. These pesticide residues would then build up in the systems of the predators. It didn't kill the birds of prey by poisoning them, but it caused complex metabolic changes. Females began to lay eggs with thin shells, which were easily crushed during incubation. Fewer chicks survived and the population plummeted.

The use of DDT was first reduced and finally banned entirely in the United States, though the chemical industry initially fought any restrictions. DDT is a persistent chemical, and it remained in the ground, still dangerous, long after its use was over. By that time the peregrine falcons had been entirely eliminated from many areas where they had once thrived. There were genuine fears that despite the DDT ban, the worldwide decline would

The peregrine falcon

continue and that the species itself would become extinct.

In the late 1960s Tom Cade, a young ornithologist, established a center for raising endangered birds of prey at Cornell University in upstate New York. Humans have had a long history of raising and training captive birds of prey. Falconry, using hawks to hunt, has been a popular sport in many parts of the world since ancient times. Cade himself had been an amateur falconer. While people had been very successful at keeping and training birds of prey, they had been much less successful at breeding them in captivity. Most trained hawks had been taken from the wild as chicks.

Cade had a particular interest in the increasingly endangered peregrine falcon. In 1971 he began a peregrine breeding program. The project was staffed by volunteers and funded by private donations. The first problem they faced was getting enough peregrine chicks to raise. The bird had already disappeared in the East. Wildlife officials were reluctant to let Cade take any wild peregrine chicks from the shrinking western population. Finally he managed to get birds from the Southwest, Alaska, Canada, and Europe. Falconers also provided the project with peregrines.

The peregrines in the program were too young to breed at first, but once they reached sexual maturity, at the age of about three, they turned out to be one of those species that breeds remarkably well in captivity. In 1973 three females laid a total of twenty-four fertile eggs. All but four of them hatched. In the wild a peregrine will normally lay a clutch of three or four eggs once a year, but they will breed again if the original clutch is lost. The trick then is to remove the first clutch of eggs, hatch them in an incubator, and let the second clutch be hatched naturally. The number of chicks in a breeding season could then be doubled. Cade and his associates were astounded at their success with double clutching. It exceeded their most optimistic expectations.

Of course there were problems that had to be solved. Peregrines are very individualistic, and each one had to be treated differently. They were also very picky about who they would accept as mates. The females tended to be larger and more aggressive, and they did most of the picking. But not always. Cade recalls one male peregrine he calls "Notorious" because he chased away all the females. But finally he was paired with a female who came from Chile. For some reason he accepted her immediately, and they became one of the most productive pairs.

By 1974 the peregrine project was ready to return birds to the wild. They decided to start in the West, where there was still a population of wild peregrines. In Colorado observers found a pair of peregrine falcons that had lost two clutches of eggs in that season. They would lay no more. First the scientists put the eggs of the more common prairie falcon into the nest so that the peregrines would not simply abandon their nest. Then they substituted two peregrine chicks from the captive breeding program. The birds seemed to accept them, and within a few weeks the chicks were flying on their own. For the first time peregrine falcons had been successfully returned to the wild.

In the East the problem would be considerably more difficult. There were no wild birds left to adopt captive-bred chicks. But over the centuries falconers had developed a technique to train their birds for hunting. The technique is called hacking. Young birds, about four weeks old, are put in a box high on a cliff or tower. In a week or two, after they have had a chance to become accustomed to their surroundings, the box is opened. The birds are then free to fly around on their own. They return to the hacking box every night to be fed. When they begin to hunt, which they do by instinct, the falconer traps them again. They are then taught to hunt on command. Tom Cade and his associates decided that they would put young birds out in the traditional way and, instead of trapping them again, just let them go.

Picking places to set up hacking stations took a great deal of thought. The location had to be safe from vandals and predators. Without adult birds to protect the nest, the young peregrines would have been very vulnerable to predators like the great horned owl. Some potentially promising sites near the sea were dropped because other conservationists feared that the endangered falcon would start preying on even more endangered species of shorebirds.

In 1975 sixteen peregrines were released. Twelve of them survived until fall—a remarkable success ratio. The birds showed themselves to be tougher and more adaptable than anyone could have hoped. Several that had been released at a military installation near Baltimore, Maryland, moved into the city, where they roosted atop office buildings and hunted pigeons.

The project was nearly derailed by federal wildlife officials over the issue of preserving and restoring only pure species. Some of the falcons being bred had come from Alaska, Canada, and Europe. They were different subspecies from the peregrine that had lived in the East. The decision to use birds from a variety of places was a deliberate one. Cade said, "We felt that was the best way to guarantee enough genetic diversity for the birds to survive and reproduce in the eastern environment." The decision had obviously been correct, for the peregrines were doing very well. Some of the captive-born birds, whose ancestors had migrated long distances, acted just like the falcons that had originally lived in the East. When the cold weather came they either stayed where they were, or migrated only a few hundred miles to warmer states. They had no irresistible instinct to migrate long distances. They simply responded to the conditions in which they found themselves.

Federal officials said that the European birds were "exotic animals," and could not by law be introduced into the country. Even the birds from Canada and the Pacific Northwest were suspect because they were of a different subspecies than the eastern peregrine falcon. Cade struck back and lined up dozens of the world's most eminent ornithologists in support of the release program. Grudgingly federal officials backed off, and the release program continued. Thousands of captive-bred peregrine falcons have now been released throughout the United States.

The captive breeding program alone did not save the peregrine falcon from extinction. The DDT ban did that. As soon as the pesticides were gone, the birds began to recover. The vast majority of the 400 or so peregrine falcons that fly over the hawk watch platform at Cape May Point each autumn are long-distance migrants and do not carry the genes of captive-bred birds. But the peregrine falcons that roost nearby do. Without the captive breeding program they never would have been able to reclaim their eastern range, and indeed expand that range into the heart of many major east coast cities.

The peregrine falcon recovery program is rightly considered one of the major successes of captive breeding.

CHAPTER 6

LEARNING TO BE WILD

AT THE NATIONAL ZOO IN WASHINGTON, D.C., I saw a tiny golden-haired monkey skitter through the trees. The monkey was not in a cage or an enclosure of any kind. Had it escaped? Not at all. The little monkey, called a golden lion tamarin, had been deliberately released in the zoo grounds so that it could learn what it is like to be a wild animal. Turning the animals loose on the zoo grounds was part of one of the most ambitious and complex captive breeding and reintroduction programs ever undertaken anywhere in the world.

By the 1970s scientists in Brazil realized that the long-term survival of this tiny monkey found mostly in the jungles was in serious jeopardy. It was often captured for medical research or for sale to the pet trade, but the most serious threat to its continued survival was the progressive destruction of its jungle habitat. There was a real, justifiable fear that the wild population would soon be so severely reduced that extinction would be inevitable.

There were a fair number of tamarins scattered throughout the world's zoos, but the survival of the captive tamarins was also threatened. Unlike many closely related species, the golden lion tamarin did not breed well in captivity. In fact it would barely breed at all, and no one knew why. In the early 1970s the plight of the captive tamarins caught the attention of Devra Kleiman of the National Zoo. She began an aggressive program to improve the little monkey's chances of survival in captivity.

The first thing to do was to find out what worked and what didn't. In the wild, golden lion tamarins were elusive and lived in the dense jungle, so authentic information about their behavior was scanty. There was a lot of information about captive tamarins, but like the animals themselves the information was scattered, and in the '70s communication between various zoos was not particularly good.

In most zoos the tamarins were kept together in fairly large groups, with several adults of each sex. That was the way most monkeys were kept, because that is how most monkeys live. But there were indications that the tamarins were different and were actually monogamous. Kleiman found that the little monkeys got along best in much smaller groups, one breeding pair and five or six of their offspring. Young tamarins learned from their parents how to care for infants.

Captive tamarins often suffered from a variety of vitamin deficiencies and other nutrition-related conditions, a result of the rigid notion that all monkeys need only fruits and vegetables. After studying all the available information on tamarins, Kleiman discovered they need protein.

The golden lion tamarin

In the wild they regularly eat insects and small animals. Once protein was added to their diet, the captive tamarins' health improved immediately. This information was shared with all zoos that kept tamarins.

With better living conditions and better nutrition, the tamarins began to breed at an almost alarming rate. Soon there were more golden lion tamarins than there were places to house them in zoos. At that point Kleiman and others began to consider seriously the possibility of using some of the captive-born tamarins to boost the declining number of wild tamarins.

The biggest challenge in all attempts to return animals to their original habitat is making sure that there is still some habitat left for them to return to. The government of Brazil had set aside some twelve thousand acres as a reserve for endangered tamarins. It was called the Poco das Antas Reserve. In the 1970s, however, the reserve existed primarily on paper. Almost half the trees in the reserve had been cut down, a railroad ran right through the center, and the land was overrun with both hunters and squatters. Perhaps one hundred tamarins clung to a precarious existence within the reserve. Clearcutting around the boundaries of the reserve had isolated the tamarins of Poco das Antas from those living in nearby areas.

The isolation of small groups is one of the less obvious dangers faced by many threatened species. Before human intervention the tamarins could range over thousands of miles of unbroken jungle, and individuals born in one area would interbreed with those born in another. Genetic diversity would be maintained. But when a habitat is fragmented, this sort of interbreeding is blocked, and when inbreeding takes place among the isolated populations, genetic diversity is lost. The health of the species suffers and if the inbreeding is severe enough, the very survival of the species can be threatened.

So while at first glance it might appear as if there were enough jungle and a sufficient number of wild tamarins in all of Brazil to insure the survival of the species, in reality their situation was far worse than it looked.

That is the main reason why the reintroduction of captive-bred tamarins seemed such a good idea. They would not only increase the total number of tamarins living in Poco das Antas, but more significantly they were unrelated to the animals already there, and would thus bring a whole new genetic heritage to the breeding stock.

Since everyone knew that it would be both difficult and expensive to bring captive-born tamarins back to the wild, it might appear that the easiest thing to do would be to trap wild tamarins living outside of Poco das Antas and turn them loose in the reserve, where they could be protected. But trapping and moving any wild animal always involves a certain amount of risk, and a certain amount of loss. Those running the tamarin rescue project felt that they couldn't afford to lose a single wild animal. But with a surplus of captive-bred tamarins, the risks and the expense would be worthwhile.

For any reintroduction project to have any chance of

success, the local population must be behind it, or at the very least not hostile to the effort. If an animal is to be protected in the wild, then its habitat has to be protected, which means land that people might use for other purposes has to be set aside for the animal's use.

In 1984 American researchers James and Lou Ann Dietz moved to the Poco das Antas Reserve to study wild tamarins and to prepare for the introduction of captive-bred animals. They knew it was essential for local people to understand what was being done and support it.

The locals had no hostility toward the tamarins themselves. They loved them and often kept them as pets, which was in itself a problem. But many did harbor hostility toward the government, which they felt had unfairly appropriated land to set up the reserve.

One thing that the Americans learned was that most of the local people, no matter how poor and uneducated, were genuinely upset about the massive deforestation of the region. Most had no idea that the tamarins were endangered, and no one had ever explained to them why the reserve was necessary in the first place. Finally some local high school students took an interest in saving tamarins. They became the heart of a campaign to reach local people, who, distrustful of outsiders for good reason, were far more likely to listen to those they knew.

The educational campaign used pamphlets, slide shows, book covers for students, and even T-shirts. Brazilian television agreed to run public service announcements about tamarins. One surprising thing the reintroduction team discovered was that most people watched television. That may not sound surprising to us, but in the Brazilian jungle most of the people didn't even have electricity. They hooked up their TVs to car batteries. In the end the campaign was successful. The residents became quite enthusiastic about saving the golden lion tamarin and saving the jungle.

The first group of twenty captive-born tamarins was released back into the wild in 1984. They had already spent months in Brazil becoming acclimated to a part of the world they had never experienced. They had received some training for their new life. For example, rather than simply presenting them with a plate of food, the researchers often hid the food so the tamarins had to hunt for it, much as they would have to do in the wild. But still the newly released tamarins did not do well. They were very reluctant to leave their cages and hunt for food. They were clumsy and fell out of trees. Instead of jumping from tree to tree as wild tamarins do, the captive-born animals would often climb down a tree, run along the ground to the next tree, and climb up. That was a great waste of energy and exposed them to predators on the ground.

Even though the researchers were on the scene and tried to protect the released tamarins and help them with supplementary food, in less than a year all but three of the original twenty animals that had been released had died or been killed. Two of the survivors were twins that had been born in the wild to a released pair.

The attempt to reintroduce captive-born tamarins to

the wild had been time-consuming, expensive, and, given the tiny survival rate, not very successful. But those involved were determined to try again. There was a good scientific reason for continuing the reintroduction project. Genetic studies of the wild tamarins in the Poco das Antas Reserve were completed in 1985 and they indicated that the animals were all very closely related. The researchers' worst fears about a severely inbred population had been confirmed. Without an influx of genetic material from unrelated tamarins, the whole population could be wiped out.

Since the greatest obstacle that the newly released animals faced was that they simply did not know how to be wild, the captive-born animals scheduled for reintroduction were given more intensive training. That's when the tamarins were released on the grounds of the National Zoo. At first the tamarins would not venture more than a few yards from their nest box. Tamarins are timid and cautious animals. But as the weeks and months passed they got bolder, and eventually ranged far enough to start examining the cages in which other zoo animals were kept. However, none of them ever tried to escape from the zoo grounds.

Elsewhere tamarins scheduled for reintroduction were kept in cages that contained a network of small branches and vines. Every few days the researchers tore up the tangled vegetation and replaced it with another network, so the animals would learn to adjust to changing conditions. The training continued even after the tamarins were released in Brazil.

All of this expensive and time-consuming effort had an effect, but only a limited effect. The trained monkeys survived for a longer period in the jungle, but they never really acted like wild tamarins. In order to be truly wild they had to be trained from birth. However, if they survived long enough to breed, there was a real payoff for all the work and expense. The wild-born offspring of captive-born parents were far better adjusted to life in the jungle, and often seemed able to teach their parents survival skills. So all in all, the golden lion tamarin release project must be considered a success.

At present the tamarin population appears to be fairly stable, and the little monkey is not in imminent danger of extinction. That is due more to habitat protection than to the reintroduction of captive-born animals, though captive breeding has certainly helped.

But one very clear lesson is that it is far easier and more efficient to save an animal in the wild than to try and put it back, once it has adjusted to captivity and forgotten how to be wild.

CHAPTER 7

RETURN OF THE UNICORN

THE ARABIAN ORYX IS A SMALL, primarily white, and beautifully marked antelope. By far its most striking features are its long, straight tapering horns, which, when viewed from the side, may look like a single horn. The ancient Egyptians raised the oryx in captivity, and sometimes may have bound the horns together so that they intertwined. Many believe that the ancient and remarkably persistent legend of the unicorn began with the Arabian oryx.

The oryx once ranged over the entire Arabian peninsula, one of the driest and most hostile places on earth. It is superbly adapted to the arid conditions because it is so efficient at extracting moisture from the plants it eats and in retaining that moisture in its body. It can go for nearly a year without drinking water. This is essential to survival in a region where a year can pass without any measurable rainfall.

Unlike most threatened animals, the oryx was not brought to the edge of extinction by the destruction of its habitat. In fact, the Arabian desert has been less altered by human intervention than most places on earth. The wild oryx was destroyed by hunting, pure and simple. At one point there were only captive oryx in the world.

Because the Arabian oryx's habitat is naturally barren, it has never been numerous. For centuries it had been hunted by the nomadic Bedouin Arabs who lived in the region, prized both for its meat and as a trophy, a proof of the hunter's skill. But the Arabian oryx was able to hold its own, even against hunters armed with rifles. The oryx is not a fast runner. In fact, it will run only for a short distance, because any greater exertion can overtax its precariously balanced system of internal temperature control and water retention. If it is forced to run for a long distance, the oryx may well die of exhaustion and dehydration. But walking, this desert antelope possesses tremendous stamina. So long as the oryx was pursued by hunters mounted on camels, it had more than an even chance, because the camels couldn't move any faster than the oryx, and the oryx would simply outwalk them. In the 1930s, however, Arab princes in the region began abandoning their traditional camels for motorized vehicles, like jeeps. The oryx could not outwalk a jeep. Even if the animal got lucky and managed to elude its pursuers, the stress of the chase would probably kill it.

Within thirty years the population of wild Arabian oryx was reduced to a remnant of less than one hundred. These hung on in the southeast end of the Arabian Peninsula, South Yemen, and a part of what is now the country of Oman known as the Jiddat-al-Harasis. The areas were remote and harsh even by the standards of the region.

But no area is so isolated that it can provide complete

protection from modern hunters. In 1961 a hunting party found several herds and killed off nearly half of the remaining wild oryx. And in 1962 there was news of further slaughters. It now appeared as if there might be as few as thirty wild oryx still alive.

Worldwide efforts to preserve endangered species were just getting started in the early 1960s. A British group dedicated to the protection of endangered species went to South Yemen to trap some of the survivors before they all were killed. They managed to corral only four oryx although one of the animals had previously been injured and subsequently died. Some believed that the four individuals captured were the last surviving wild representatives of their species. It turned out that there were still a few wild oryx, but these too were soon killed by hunters.

Since there were no protected wildlife reserves within the oryx's old home territory, there was no point in putting the three captured animals back, where they would undoubtedly fall prey to hunters almost immediately. But where to put them? After a good deal of discussion among wildlife protection groups, the oryx were sent to a zoo in Phoenix, Arizona. The desert climate of the American Southwest would be familiar to them. There weren't enough animals to start a breeding program, but the new captives were soon joined by seven others from the London Zoo and from private collections in Kuwait and Saudi Arabia. These formed the nucleus for what was to be called the World Herd.

Arabian oryx

The Arabian oryx turned out to be a wonderful subject for a captive breeding and reintroduction program, for a variety of reasons. The first was that plant eaters such as antelopes, deer, wild sheep and goats, and the like generally seem to do much better in captivity than most other types of animals. What they need primarily is space, and in Arizona they had plenty of that.

The Arabian oryx had been kept in captivity since the time of the ancient Egyptians, so a good deal was known about how to keep them successfully. Ever since it became apparent that the oryx was headed for extinction in the wild, some Arabian noblemen had begun keeping their own private herds, supposedly for conservation purposes. In fact, they were building their own herds by capturing wild animals but not breeding them effectively. Thus they were really depleting the wild stock of the animals they claimed to be trying to save. Still, by the time the oryx actually disappeared from the wild, there were a fair number of them in captivity. No one was quite sure how many, and it was feared that some of the privately held herds were dangerously inbred. But there were a sufficient number of captive Arabian oryx, which assured researchers of their ability to survive in zoos and private reserves.

The World Herd began producing calves in 1963. By sheer chance all of the first six calves born were male. Biologists breathed a hearty sigh of relief when the seventh calf, born in 1966, was a female. After that the animals began reproducing so rapidly that the herd was divided among a number of different institutions, including the famous San Diego Wild Animal Park. The animals were relocated partly for reasons of space, but primarily to ensure that the captive stock would not be wiped out by a local epidemic or natural disaster.

By the 1970s great changes had taken place in the Arabian oryx's former home range. The reason for the changes can be explained in a single word—oil. The Arabian Peninsula was found to contain huge deposits of oil. The desert was now littered with oil wells and crossed by pipelines. The price of oil had also risen dramatically, and regions that had once been among the poorest in the world suddenly became among the wealthiest.

The kings, emirs, and sultans who had encouraged the changes and profited most handsomely from them had also become very uneasy about the rapid pace of change. They feared that traditional ways of life that had endured for centuries might be swept away, leaving people without roots.

In 1974 the sultan of Oman decided that it might be a good idea to try to restore the Arabian oryx—a symbol of the desert and, in a sense, a symbol of an ancient way of life—to the Jiddat-al-Harasis, which lay within his domain. He let it be known that he would personally fund such a project. Most reintroduction projects operate on a shoestring, with, at best, the indifferent support of local authorities. This time money would be no problem, and in Oman the sultan's word was law. Once again the Arabian oryx was lucky.

The headquarters for what came to be called Operation Oryx was set up at a place called Yalooni. It was nearly two hundred miles from the nearest settlement, and temperatures varied from an average of hotter than 110 degrees Fahrenheit in the summer, to the 40s in the winter. Yalooni was remote, rugged, and inhospitable even for the Arabian Peninsula.

The region was certainly a desert, but it was more than a vast expanse of shifting sand, which first comes to mind when we hear the word desert. Much of it was a flat rocky plain, where grasses and shrubs grew. In rainy years—rainy for that part of the world—the vegetation was fairly plentiful.

While there were no permanent residents of this region, a nomadic people called the Harasis did graze their goats in the region. The Harasis posed a potential problem for the oryx because their goats might destroy the forage the oryx would need, particularly in a dry year. But they were also potentially beneficial. The Harasis' traditional way of life was being eroded by the oil boom. The plan was to employ some of the Harasis men, who knew the desert better than anyone else, to work as guards to protect the oryx against poachers. The Harasis were enthusiastic about the prospect. Unlike going to work in the oil fields, this sort of work allowed them to maintain at least a part of their old way of life. And the Harasis had always looked upon the oryx as a symbol of the desert, and were glad to see its return. It was not difficult to persuade them to keep their goats away from areas that were being grazed by oryx.

A million-dollar facility was constructed at Yalooni so that the oryx could be acclimated before they were turned loose. It included pens and an enclosed 250-acre grazing area. There was enough space for the captive-born oryx, initially only fourteen of them, to develop normal herd behavior before going off on their own. If reintroduction stations were hotels, this one for the oryx was the Ritz.

The climate suited the oryx quite nicely. They preferred the natural grasses and other vegetation to the hay they had grown up with. After some initial scuffling among the males, the newly formed herd settled down happily in their large enclosed home. The only concern among the people running the project was water. In captivity the oryx were regularly supplied with water. Would the captive-born animals be able to do without water for long periods, as their wild ancestors had?

The gates to the enclosure were opened in January 1982, and the oryx herd placidly wandered out. At first they stayed fairly close to the pens, but as time went on they began to extend their range. Their progress was followed by about a dozen Harasis nomads, who had been hired to keep track of the herd and protect them from any hunters. Much to the relief of those in charge of the project, the newly released oryx seemed to have little need for water. The herd soon took up the wandering life of the wild oryx.

When they finally did return to the area in which they had once been penned, almost two years had passed. The region was in the midst of one of its periodic droughts, and the oryx may have been trying to find supplementary food and water. But another newly released herd was already in that area. The leaders of the two herds fought to determine dominance, and then split up the territory. The herds received supplementary food during the two-year drought, but when the rains came, and the grasses and shrubs again grew in the desert, the oryx wandered off and established new territories elsewhere.

In the years that followed, more captive-bred oryx from the World Herd were released into the desert, primarily to increase the genetic diversity of the herds. And the oryx have flourished. Their dependence on human intervention seems to have been broken completely. As far as anyone can determine they are now indistinguishable from the thousands of generations of wild-born oryx. But every single oryx that is now roaming free in the desert was either born in captivity or is the direct descendant of a captive-born animal.

Though the total population of free-ranging Arabian oryx is still dangerously low, just a few hundred, and the range limited, everyone connected with the oryx reintroduction project regards it as an unqualified success and a model for all future captive breeding and reintroduction projects.

Programs to reintroduce the Arabian oryx are now underway in other Middle Eastern countries, like Saudi Arabia, Israel, and Jordan. At present zoos still provide an important backup for the oryx. There are still more Arabian oryx in captivity than in the wild—more than 300 animals scattered among twenty zoos. If some new disaster strikes the wild population, the species will not disappear. And zoo visitors have a chance to view this rare and beautiful animal in person.

The Harasis have proved to be exceptionally good at their job of tracking and protecting the animals, and they appear to genuinely enjoy the work. An enormous amount has been learned about the life of the now wild Arabian oryx. This information is not only useful in helping to manage the Arabian oryx successfully, but in helping to preserve and promote the well-being of other similar animals.

The success of Operation Oryx is the result of a number of factors: dedication, more than ample funding, a cooperative human population, good luck, and the nature of the oryx itself, which, unlike most captive-born animals, was able to leave the security of its cage almost without a backward glance.

CHAPTER 8

THE SYMBOL

THE GIANT PANDA is probably the most popular animal in the whole world. There is something almost magical about the appeal of this lumbering, bearlike creature with the distinctive black-and-white markings. Most children have owned a toy panda. The panda is instantly recognizable to billions of people throughout the world, yet very few humans have seen a living representative of the species, and for a good reason: there are very few living pandas. Fewer than a thousand may survive in the remote bamboo forests of China. A far smaller number are kept in captivity, mostly in China.

The panda is the symbol of the World Wildlife Fund (WWF), which, for the last twenty years, has been the leading international organization for the preservation of endangered species. There has been more time, effort, and money devoted to saving the severely endangered panda, than to saving any other single species. As much as any other, the panda story illustrates the promise and the shortcomings, even the potential dangers, of captive breeding.

The giant panda has always been rare. It was first "discovered," that is, made known to the outside world, in 1896 by a French missionary in China. Su-Lin, the first panda to leave China, was brought to New York in 1936, and the following year it was acquired by Chicago's Brookfield Zoo. A panda craze started, and it continues today. There were panda dolls, panda cartoons, and lots of other panda merchandise. Su-Lin died of pneumonia a little over a year after being brought to Chicago, but he was followed by two other pandas, the last of which died in 1953.

I grew up in Chicago and vividly remember trips to the zoo to see the panda, which was housed in a large, circular, outdoor cage. I even recall slipping under the guardrail and getting close enough to put my fingers through the wire mesh to touch the back of a sleeping panda. That is something that would not be possible today, and was never a good idea. Despite their toylike appearance, pandas do not like to be bothered, and they have a bad temper. Adult males can weigh up to 300 pounds, and are extremely strong. Pandas have inflicted serious injuries on zookeepers and are considered among the most dangerous of all zoo animals.

Pandas were sent to a number of other zoos in the United States, and in addition to Brookfield, and to other parts of the world. But after World War II the strained relations between the West and the new Communist government in China brought an end to the panda trade. That was probably a good thing because capturing these popular animals for zoos helped to deplete the already small stock of wild pandas, and at that time there was little serious thought given to breeding pandas in captivity. In Chicago, for example, a "mate" was bought for its male panda—but it turned out to be another male.

By the 1960s China began to break out of its political isolation, and it used pandas as "goodwill ambassadors." After President Richard Nixon visited China, the Chinese government sent two pandas to the National Zoo in Washington, D.C. They became instant stars and probably did more to improve relations between China and the United States than dozens of planeloads of diplomats shuttling back and forth.

Zoos in London, Mexico City, and a small number of other Western cities received pandas from China. Wherever the pandas were displayed, crowds would gather around the panda enclosure just to watch the animals sleep—which is what pandas do most of the time.

In 1987 a pair of pandas were on temporary loan to the Bronx Zoo in New York. Before the exhibit officially opened, a special viewing was arranged for members of the zoo. The Bronx Zoo has lots of members, and interest was so high that several special viewings had to be scheduled. On the evening I attended, there were about one thousand of us standing around the enclosure, watching a panda sleep. Then suddenly it got up and began to waddle clumsily around the enclosure. That was the first time, since I had been a child back in Chicago, that I had actually seen a living panda move. I was completely captivated. For me the animal had lost none of its magic.

The giant panda

What has this obvious star quality, this celebrity status, done for the continued survival of the panda? The picture is decidedly a mixed one. Since the WWF adopted the panda as its symbol, that organization and other international conservation organizations have poured millions of dollars into China to aid in the preservation of the panda in the wild and to encourage a captive breeding program. China is a poor and badly overpopulated country that has undergone wars, revolutions, and vast social upheaval throughout much of the twentieth century. Though many in China were extremely interested in panda preservation, for the Chinese consider the giant panda a national treasure, they had little experience in this sort of conservation effort and even less money with which to face the truly formidable problems.

The international project to save the panda had troubles from the start. There were scientific problems: Because so little is known about the panda and how it lives, it was often difficult to know what to do to help it. There were political difficulties because the Chinese simply did not trust outsiders who tried to tell them what to do. China's own enormous bureaucracy was often at odds with itself. And there were cultural differences: For example the Chinese often felt that it was in the best interest of the panda simply to capture the animal and put it in a nice comfortable cage, rather than let it face the dangers of the wild. Conservationists in the West now believe that it is best to make every effort to keep an animal in the wild if at all possible.

In mid 1990 Prince Philip of England, president of the WWF and a man known for speaking bluntly, gave a gloomy assessment of what the organization had accomplished with all the money it had spent trying to protect the panda.

He said that the results were "disappointing" and that the organization never should have poured a lot of money into China. The big problem, the prince said, was that the Chinese were cutting down the bamboo forests that the panda needed for survival.

"Unfortunately, in spite of WWF spending a fortune on it, the chances of the panda surviving at the present rate of progress are not good."

Stung by the criticism the Chinese shot back that the WWF had no right to interfere in China's affairs, that they had used the panda symbol to raise millions of dollars and had sent only a small portion of that money to China. These arguments had been going on for years.

The greatest long-term threat to panda survival is destruction of habitat. Though the places where pandas live are generally remote and inhospitable for humans, people and pandas do share the area, and the human population is growing. Pandas are adapted to eating bamboo and nothing else. If the bamboo goes, so will the pandas. But the bamboo is of no use to farmers. They cut down the bamboo forests the pandas need to survive. The Chinese government has made efforts to move people out of specially designated panda preserves, but that isn't easy in overcrowded China. Such plans are often denounced as placing the welfare of animals above that of people, and they are frequently ignored by local officials who are not necessarily very enthusiastic about saving pandas when it means closing off land that could be used for farming.

Poaching is a more immediate threat. Though it is strictly illegal to kill any wild panda in China today, panda pelts fetch a high price on the black market. Panda furs are status symbols in Hong Kong, Taiwan, and Japan. While it may seem incredible that anyone would encourage the killing of this severely endangered species, there are those who will pay more than ten thousand dollars for a single fur. A live panda sold on the black market to a private collector can bring well over one hundred thousand dollars. That kind of money has proved too great a temptation for poor Chinese farmers who live near the panda's home.

At first China did not handle the poaching problem very well. Before 1987 the penalties against illegally killing a panda were fairly light with a maximum of two years in jail, and these were rarely applied. There were no penalties at all for smuggling or selling the skins. Then the Chinese got serious. They proclaimed that those convicted of killing a panda or smuggling even a single panda skin could be sentenced to prison for ten or more years, life imprisonment, or could even get the death penalty. This is no idle threat. People have been executed for panda poaching, and many more are serving long prison sentences under harsh conditions.

That helped but did not eliminate the problem because

the potential financial rewards were so great. "I couldn't earn that much in a lifetime. Even though I risked my life, it was worth it," a poacher was quoted as telling police. "If you hadn't caught me, I would have been rich."

Ironically, the panda's best friends have sometimes turned out to be their worst enemies. Early panda enthusiasts were so anxious to provide specimens for zoos that they simply overlooked the brutal and often deadly methods used to capture the animals, and the fact that many captive pandas did not survive for long. Those days are gone, hopefully forever. Pandas are no longer captured indiscriminately for display in zoos. But zoologist George Schaller, who spent years studying the panda and knows more about the animal than anyone outside of China, says there are still too many of these rare animals taken from the wild for display.

The Chinese government no longer hands out pandas as rewards to countries that are friendly to them. But pandas are in such demand by zoos throughout the world that the Chinese loaned them out for temporary display, at a price—usually a very steep price. Wherever a panda appears, the crowds are sure to follow. People pay admission, buy souvenirs, and provide badly needed funds for the zoo. The zoos pay the Chinese, who use the money to pay for their own panda protection projects.

The Chinese were making enormous sums of money out of what came to be called derisively the "rent-a-panda" program. They were approving requests for pandas not only from zoos, but from state fairs, even supermarket chains. Clearly the program had become a strictly commercial venture, and a profitable one. The Chinese government was encouraged to capture more pandas or disrupt their own captive breeding programs by sending animals on long and stressful journeys. The money made from panda loans was supposed to go entirely to panda conservation, but many who were familiar with the Chinese programs suspected that this was not so, and that the money that did go to panda programs was not being spent very well.

During the late 1980s a tremendous controversy erupted over panda loan programs. Most zoo professionals and conservation organizations urged that the loan program be shut down at least temporarily, until a comprehensive panda protection program could be worked out. But the pressures to get a panda for exhibit are enormous.

It is hard for ordinary zoogoers to accept that for the time being, it is far better for the pandas to remain in China, and preferably in their remote bamboo forest homes, where we will probably never be able to go and see them. But that's how it is.

It would seem that captive breeding would be ideal for the giant panda. Certainly a thriving captive population of pandas would provide a much needed backup for the small and severely threatened wild population. And close observation of captive pandas could vastly increase our knowledge of how pandas live, and that knowledge could be used to help protect the wild population. Pandas appear to do well in captivity—that is, most captive pandas live long and healthy lives. Being relatively slow-moving and solitary creatures, they do not seem to suffer from the stresses of captivity as do more high-strung and wide-ranging creatures.

But there is one problem—a big one. Pandas are extremely difficult to breed in captivity.

For years the United States media followed the agonizing and ultimately unsuccessful attempts to breed the pandas at Washington's National Zoo. Pandas have been bred successfully only in China and, strangely, in Mexico, but the survival rate of captive-born animals has been low. The captive population has not been able to reproduce itself, which means that wild pandas must still be caught to supply zoos and captive breeding projects. The captive breeding program in China remains primitive and haphazard by Western standards.

Most captive-panda births are the results of artificial insemination. Just why it is so hard to breed captive pandas remains a mystery. We have had very little experience with captive pandas, and we know so little about panda behavior in general that the problems are not really surprising. With time and effort they certainly can be solved, as they have with other once-difficult-to-breed species, like the gorilla. The fear is that with so few pandas left, time is running out.

But in the last few years the pandas' survival prospects have begun to look better. The future of the giant panda has always been in the hands of the Chinese people. And they now seem to be taking panda conservation much more seriously than in the past.

In 1993 there was a huge "panda festival" in China. Also a number of new panda sanctuaries have been established, with promises of more to come. Those who staff the reserves are now more motivated and knowledgeable. Field studies indicate that the wild panda population has stabilized in many areas. The Chinese government is now beginning to look seriously at the possibilities of panda tourism—that is, bringing tourists and their money into areas where they could see wild pandas. That would make free-living pandas far more valuable to the local people than panda pelts sold on the black market. Right now you have to be very hardy and very rich to travel to any of the panda reserves, for there are few tourist facilities and everything is expensive, but soon that may change. It's possible that the wild pandas, which are now wary of people, may become familiar enough with visitors to show themselves more frequently. This has been the pattern at the more successful African animal preserves.

There is even good news on the captive breeding front. Susan Minka of the WWF said in 1994, "In the past five years, the survival rate [in China's captive-panda breeding program] has passed 50 percent." There may soon be captive-born animals to send overseas. Most major zoos in the United States and elsewhere will now accept only captive-born animals for exhibit. When they become available they will generate millions of dollars for panda preservation in China. So you may yet have a chance to see a real live panda.

It's naive to be too optimistic about the future of any species as severely endangered as the giant panda. But at least there are some grounds for hope that this symbol of all endangered species, and most engaging-looking of all animals, may yet survive.

CHAPTER 9

A DIFFERENT BREED OF CAT

THE CHEETAH, whose range is now limited to Africa and a tiny population in Asia, may actually have originated in what is now North America. One hundred thousand years ago, or so, four distinct species of cheetah roamed much of the northern hemisphere and Africa.

Then some ten to twelve thousand years ago, at the end of the geologic period called the Pleistocene, something terrible happened to the cheetah, along with most of the world's large mammals. They died off in enormous numbers. The mammoth, the mastodon, and the saber-toothed cat disappeared completely. So did the giant sloth and the glyptodon, a South American armadillo the size of a small automobile. Some 80 percent of the large mammals of North and South America did not survive. The die-off of large mammals in Europe and Asia was nearly as severe. Africa, which is still the home of the most diverse population of large mammals was not hit as severely. But even Africa had a greater range of species before the Pleistocene extinctions. No one knows the reason for this wave of extinctions. Everything from climate changes to disease to the appearance of human hunters using fire has been suggested.

Many of those species that did not entirely disappear had their ranges severely altered and their total numbers reduced. The horse and camel, both of which first evolved in North America, disappeared from the Western Hemisphere, but survived and ultimately thrived in Asia and Africa. The horse was brought back to North America by the Spanish.

The cheetah also became extinct in North America, but survived in Africa and Asia. Its total numbers had been dangerously reduced. At one point there may have been only a few breeding pairs of cheetahs left in the entire world. The cheetahs, however, made a comeback. Their numbers increased and they once again became well established in Africa and parts of Asia, though they never returned to the Western Hemisphere. Now, however, there was only a single species of cheetah, divided into a few subspecies that looked almost identical.

The cheetah is very definitely a different breed of cat. It is a member of the feline family, but it has a genus *Acinonyx* all to itself. There is only one species, *jubatus*. Your house cat is more closely related to the mighty lion than is the cheetah, which shares the African grasslands with the lion and can weigh up to 100 pounds.

If you watch your own cat, and then watch a lion in the zoo or see a video of a lion in Africa, the similarity is obvious and striking. There are the same fluid motions, the same stalking moves as they approach their prey. The

The cheetah

cheetah, on the other hand, has a proportionally smaller head, longer legs, and a rangier body than a lion or a house cat. It trots rather than glides, and when it runs with enormous body-stretching strides, there is nothing quite like it on earth. It is the fastest of all land animals, and in short bursts can reach speeds of up to seventy miles per hour. The cheetah will run down a speedy gazelle, instead of stalking its prey and pouncing on it at the last moment, like the lion, tiger, and house cat. Typically, wolves and wild dogs run down their prey, and for that reason the cheetah is considered the most doglike of all the cats. Unlike every other member of the cat family, the cheetah does not have retractable claws.

In historic times the cheetah population suffered another very serious blow. Unlike lions and tigers and other big cats, the cheetah can be tamed. It could never be a house pet, it can't even really be domesticated like a dog, but like a falcon it can be trained for hunting. Other large cats are so naturally aggressive that they remain a constant threat to their trainers, but the trained cheetah is not dangerously aggressive. Cheetahs were once popularly called hunting leopards, though they are not leopards, despite having spots.

Tame cheetahs were known in the days of the pharaohs of Egypt. Between the fourteenth and sixteenth centuries, they were widely used for hunting in Central Asia and India. Akbar the Great, a sixteenth-century Mogul emperor of India, had some 9,000 hunting cheetahs during his reign, and he was just one of many rulers or wealthy individuals who kept cheetahs. These animals were prized, but they did not breed well in captivity. Indeed, they practically didn't breed at all. According to records, Akbar's enormous herd of tame cheetahs produced only one live birth. That meant that virtually every captive cheetah had to be taken from the wild, which put a huge drain on the wild cheetah population.

By the beginning of the twentieth century, the cheetah, like all big cats, was intensively hunted by people who wanted furs and trophies. Though cheetahs were no longer used for hunting, like other big cats they were in demand for display in zoos. Once again there was an enormous drain on the wild cheetah population.

In more recent years the most serious threat to cheetah survival has been habitat destruction. A growing human population has been moving in on land that was once the cheetah's hunting ground. The cheetah can present a threat to cattle and other livestock. The world's wild cheetah population lives mainly in Africa and may consist of only fifteen thousand individuals. It is broken up into small and isolated pockets, which makes the animals' situation even more precarious. The cheetah faces the same competition with humans that is faced by most of the world's large mammals. But for the cheetah, captivity has provided a very tenuous refuge from extinction.

Most wild cats, large and small, breed very well in captivity. Even in the bad old days of zoos, when lions and tigers were kept in tiny, barred, concrete cages, they still would breed prolifically. There are far more captive-born lions than there are good zoos with space to keep the lions. Today the wild tiger is being hunted to extinction in its Asian homeland, but there would be plenty of captive-born tigers to reintroduce to the wild, if there were any wild left in which to reintroduce them. Unfortunately there is not. Even the rare and elusive snow leopard, which was virtually unknown in captivity until a decade or two ago, is now being successfully bred in a number of zoos throughout the world. But not the cheetah. And that is a problem that has puzzled zoologists for a long time now.

The extraordinary difficulty of breeding cheetahs in captivity can be dramatically demonstrated by noting that after the birth of a cheetah cub in Akbar's collection back in the sixteenth century, the second known captive birth came in 1956 in the Philadelphia Zoo. While the breeding record has improved in the last forty years, it has not improved all that much. And that is really surprising, since humans have had such a long history of keeping cheetahs in captivity.

In 1975 the Endangered Species Act banned the importation of a number of wild-caught species, the cheetah included. Since zoos could no longer replace these popular exhibits with wild-caught specimens, there was a new emphasis on captive breeding and the problems of breeding cheetahs. Many zoos tried to breed cheetahs, but fewer than half succeeded. In 1987 only fifty-two individuals, fewer than 15 percent of the cheetah population in American zoos, had been bred successfully. At that time two-thirds of all the cheetahs born in American zoos were descended from ten individuals. At that rate the captive population appeared to be in far greater danger than the threatened wild population.

Male cheetahs show unusually low sperm counts and other abnormalities when compared to other cats. And among captive cheetahs there seemed to be an exceptionally high percentage of stillbirths and birth defects. All of this suggested a population that was suffering from the problems of severe inbreeding. But what about those wild-caught cheetahs that were not breeding at all? What was wrong with them?

During the 1980s scientists from the National Cancer

Institute began to do genetic research on cheetahs. The findings were quite remarkable. In one study of 200 DNA sequences from fifty-five cheetahs, they found less than one percent variation among individuals. Humans in comparable genetic studies vary in 32 percent of the gene sites, cats in 21 percent, lions in 12 percent, ocelots in 20 percent. Of 250 species studied for genetic variations, the average variability is about 36 percent. Researchers say that cheetahs show the kind of variability that could be expected in laboratory mice after ten to twenty generations of brother-sister matings. It didn't make any difference whether the cheetah was born in the zoo or on the African plains; all cheetahs were virtually identical genetically. The entire species was inbred, and had been for a long time.

That brings us back to the history of the cheetah, described at the start of this chapter. Scientists believe that the cheetah passed through one, and possibly two, "genetic bottlenecks." These were times when the population was reduced to a few individuals. While the total population rebounded, genetic variability had been lost. The cheetah had become naturally inbred.

One of the characteristics of a severely inbred population is a low birthrate. Another is susceptibility to disease. In previous chapters I have mentioned how captive populations are often split up among different zoos and institutions to guard against the possibility that an epidemic might wipe out all the members of a species in one place. In 1982 that sort of disaster hit a successful cheetah breeding program at the Wildlife Safari Park in Oregon. The disease was feline infectious peritonitis. It had first been identified in domestic cats in 1966 and was fatal to about one percent of all the cats exposed to it. But it killed 60 percent of the park's forty-two cheetahs, and infected the rest. The lions at the park were also exposed, but none of them even showed symptoms.

Since the early 1980s the cheetah has been the subject of more high-tech genetic studies than any other wild animal. When I visited the cheetah center at the Cincinnati Zoo recently, all of the animals had large, shaved patches on their undersides. I was told that they had just been given thorough examinations, which required taking both blood samples and tissue biopsies.

NOHAS (New Opportunities in Animal Health Sciences) of the National Zoo uses a mobile lab to transport, from one zoo to another, sophisticated laboratory instruments that help researchers learn more about the reproductive biology of the cheetah. Artificial insemination, hormone treatments, and just about every other modern scientific technique for boosting the fertility of this endangered cat have been tried. There have been some successes, but no breakthroughs. Despite the best efforts of science, the birthrate among captive cheetahs remains dangerously low.

All of these highly sophisticated treatments and the concentration on the scientifically fashionable subject of genetics have produced something of a backlash among some scientists and zoo professionals. The cheetah's problems, they believe, are not so much in the genes as in their living conditions.

In the early 1990s some zoologists began taking a new and in-depth look at cheetah breeding problems. It was clear that most captive male cheetahs had abnormal sperm counts. But average sperm counts of male cheetahs differed widely among zoos. Also, neither sperm count nor any other known reproductive trait appeared to distinguish male cheetahs who were successful breeders from those who were not.

An even more surprising finding was that wild cheetahs were breeding quite freely, though their genetic makeup was virtually identical to that of the captive cheetahs. In some places the number of wild cheetahs was actually increasing. They were in trouble in areas where larger and more aggressive lions were expanding their range and where the habitat for their chief food source, gazelles, was being destroyed. The problem for the wild cheetahs was competition and a shrinking food supply, not their genes.

A closer look at the records of captive-born cheetahs shattered the idea that they produced an exceptionally large number of stillborn or seriously ill cubs. While they did not do as well as lions, cheetah cubs had a survival record comparable to that of snow leopards and clouded leopards. The previous records had been deceptive because most of the abnormal births had come from a single female. The new look at the statistics did not support the idea that cheetahs were a group of animals suffering from the results of severe inbreeding.

"The simpler explanation is that we don't know how to breed cheetahs well," said Oliver A. Ryder, a geneticist at the Zoological Society of San Diego.

For a long time most zoos kept cheetahs in the big-cat house, next to the lions and tigers. But as soon as the cheetahs were moved to isolated quarters of their own, reproductive success increased. It seems that they were simply being intimidated by the larger and stronger felines.

Usually zoos paired a single male and female cheetah. But in the wild cheetahs live in small groups. Zoos had already learned that the breeding success of gorillas could be increased dramatically when they were kept in large groups, which is how they live in the wild. On the other hand golden lion tamarins, once kept in large colonies, did much better in small family units. The key for breeding the cheetah, as it has been for these other animals, may be to try to reproduce natural living conditions as closely as possible.

Some researchers have even begun to question whether the cheetah's lack of genetic diversity makes it more sensitive to outbreaks of disease. The classic case was the 1982 epidemic at the Wildlife Safari in Winston, Oregon. "We have to assume that the [Oregon cheetah] population was also naive [previously unexposed to the virus]," says James F. Evermann, a microbiologist at Washington State University. If so, then these animals were like American Indians who succumbed to measles and smallpox brought over by European newcomers. "Nobody says that was from inbreeding," Ryder notes.

Since the 1982 outbreak, the cheetahs appear to be developing an immunity to the virus. The virus accounted for just three cheetah deaths between 1987 and 1991. The number of cheetahs with antibodies to the virus has risen dramatically.

A fear of catastrophic epidemics still exists. The 800 or so captive cheetahs in the United States are scattered in more than 130 zoos and wildlife parks. Extreme caution is exercised in shipping cheetahs from one place to another, for fear that they might carry some dangerous virus. But the overhanging dread of a doomsday epidemic, which was so prevalent just a few years ago, has receded somewhat.

Some researchers now feel that the theory that inbreeding would cause the inevitable and rapid extinction of the cheetah was greatly exaggerated. The cheetah is not the only species that shows little genetic diversity. Some species seem to tolerate inbreeding fairly well, while others do not. The cheetah may actually be one of those species that is not seriously harmed by limited genetic diversity.

Stephen J. O'Brien of the National Cancer Institute, who led the original genetic analysis of the cheetah, notes that it appears as if cheetahs have lacked genetic diversity for about 10,000 years. "If that's the case, the cheetah has gone through a number of generations—several thousand, actually—without dying [out]. It's very encouraging."

Eventually the reproductive problems plaguing the

captive cheetahs may be overcome, and a self-sustaining population created. Eventually it might even be possible to return captive-bred animals to their natural habitat to boost declining numbers in the wild.

Reintroduction of captive-born cheetahs is still a long way off. But at present it does not look as if the fastest land animal in the world is genetically doomed.

CHAPTER 10

THE HIGH-TECH ZOO

AT THE SAN DIEGO ZOO, and a couple of other major zoos in the United States, there are small rooms that have been referred to in the press and on television as "frozen zoos." They have been popularly hailed as a new way to save endangered species. This sort of description conjures up all sorts of science fiction images: In the twenty-first century, previously frozen animals that have long been extinct are thawed out, and once again put into zoos or released back into the wild. The image is that of a sort of Jurassic Park with rhinos and cheetahs rather than dinosaurs.

Reality is not quite as startling. What are being preserved in these cryonics, or low temperature laboratories, are frozen sperm, eggs, and occasionally frozen embryos of endangered species. There is nothing really new about this technology. It has been used successfully for many years with cattle, horses, and even purebred dogs. The same techniques are also increasingly used in human fertility clinics.

The frozen zoo concept is a very practical one for many

endangered animals. Here is an example: Let us say that for genetic reasons, it was decided that a particular endangered African elephant kept in a zoo in Atlanta should be mated with another in the Portland, Oregon, zoo. Shipping an elephant clear across the country is extremely expensive, difficult, and inevitably quite stressful for the animal. Some delicate species will not breed if they are moved too frequently or too far. The trip may even kill them. Shipping frozen sperm or a frozen embryo is much easier and cheaper, and it works with elephants, rhinos, and a lot of other species.

Then there is simply the matter of space. As I noted in the very first chapter, all of the professionally run zoos in the world could fit into an area of about seventy square miles. The American Zoo and Aquarium Association (AZA) estimates that even if all the space is used to utmost efficiency, North American zoos and aquariums have the capacity to sustain only about 900 species. "Considering that over 2,000 vertebrates will probably require captive breeding to save them from extinction, 900 is not a large number. Preserving the genetic material of many animals in 'frozen zoos' may greatly increase the number of species that can be saved," says an official AZA publication. Frozen zoos will certainly allow for greater genetic diversity in a breeding program, without increasing the number of individual animals in the program beyond the zoos' capacity to handle them.

Probably the most spectacular results from the use of advanced reproductive technology with an endangered species were obtained with the gaur, the largest of all wild cattle. The gaur, which is found in the lowland rain forests of India, Burma, and Malaysia, is rapidly being hunted and squeezed out of existence in the wild.

Since the population of gaur in nature is so low, it is considered unwise to remove any more wild animals to supplement the captive population. But the captive population was bred from only nine gaur—a situation that could easily lead to severe genetic problems down the road. The solution has been to collect semen from wild gaur and, through artificial insemination, introduce new genetic material into the captive population without taking any animals out of the wild. The first successful use of this technique came in July 1989, when a female gaur calf was born at Omaha's Henry Doorly Zoo as the result of artificial insemination with semen collected and frozen nearly two years before.

In 1981 there was a well publicized gaur birth at the Bronx Zoo. The calf was born to a Holstein cow through an embryo transfer. This event has been hailed as a triumph and a breakthrough for captive breeding. The significance of the event was this: The gaur is rare and sometimes difficult to manage in captivity; the cow is common and easy to handle. The cow can be more closely watched by zoo veterinarians. There are many endangered species that do produce fertile embryos, but for one reason or another have difficulty giving birth successfully. If embryos could be transferred to closely related species that could bear the young, this would open a lot of possibilities.

The gaur

Simply keeping endangered animals healthy in zoos presents an enormous challenge. A great deal is known about keeping familiar animals—lions, hippos and the like—in zoos. Large numbers of them have been kept for a long time. Many of the threatened species, however, are not only rare in the wild, they are rare in zoos as well. They can have health problems that were solved long ago among more common species.

In the chapter on the golden lion tamarin, for example, the problems with its diet were explained. Once those diet problems were solved by zoos sharing information and experiences, the health of the captive tamarin population improved greatly.

The red panda is the closest relative of the giant panda,

though it looks a lot more like a raccoon than the famous black-and-white variety. Like its celebrated relative, the red panda is adapted to eating primarily bamboo, as well as the leaves, buds, shoots, and fruits of other plants. But the nutritional needs of the red panda were poorly understood until 1986, when those in charge of the Species Survival Plan for the red panda, in conjunction with the National Zoo, began an intensive study of red panda nutrition. The diets of all the red pandas in North American zoos were examined.

Every zoo seemed to have its own favorite diet, but as a result of the study, a nutritionally complete artificial diet has been developed. The result is a commercially produced food called a "panda bisket."

Today the health, appearance, activity, and reproduction of captive red pandas have been completely changed. Before the development of the "panda bisket," most captive red pandas had dull coats, were sluggish, prone to disease, and did not reproduce well. With the new diet the red panda has gone from being an animal that did poorly in captivity to one that appears to thrive.

Red pandas can now be moved more easily from one zoo to another, because wherever they go they get the same standardized diet. The standardization of the "panda bisket" has also helped to expand the number of zoos that can house this engaging creature. At one time pandas were limited to zoos that had access to a regular supply of bamboo—usually zoos in warm climates, where bamboo grows. Shipping large quantities of bamboo can be prohibitively expensive.

The threatened maned wolf of South America has a diet of small mammals, and a fondness for domestic chickens (which gets it into a lot of trouble). In addition this unusual animal eats a large quantity of a tomatolike fruit called lobeira. That's a singular diet for a wolf. In captivity maned wolves were fed a typical wolf diet, though it did include the lobeira, which is unavailable to most North American zoos.

The maned wolf does not do well in zoos. It is highly susceptible to a serious and often fatal urinary condition, and scientists believe that this is due to a diet problem, possibly the lack of lobeira. A number of zoos are conducting research to see if some changes in the diet will help solve the problem. The health difficulties of the maned wolf are typical of those that face many endangered species in captivity. There are so few of these animals that we just don't know enough about them. Would anyone imagine that a wolf could get sick because it wasn't eating enough fruit?

Usually scientists learn about the behavior of animals by observing them in the wild. The lessons learned can then be applied to keeping that species in captivity. But with some endangered species there are so few remaining in the wild, or they live in such remote and inaccessible places, that field studies of behavior are difficult or impossible.

Take the case of Matschiei's tree kangaroo, one of a group of kangaroos that is adapted to living in trees. Limited field observations led to the conclusion that these rare kangaroos lived in "harems" consisting of an adult male and several females and their offspring, so that is the way they were kept in zoos. But it wasn't working. The kangaroos would breed, but then the joeys (infant kangaroos) were often found dead and no one could figure out why.

Then tree kangaroos were placed at the National Zoo's Conservation and Research Center at Fort Royal, Virginia, and Seattle's Woodland Park Zoo, where they had enough space to arrange their own living conditions. Close observation of the animals in a relatively natural setting indicated that tree kangaroos are really quite antisocial. Adult females live in their own exclusive territories, and are extremely aggressive toward one another. In some cases they have actually been seen pulling joeys from another female's pouch.

The solution to this problem was a simple one. Female tree kangaroos with joeys are now completely isolated from other adult tree kangaroos.

One problem with touting the success of captive breeding programs, and particularly such high-tech concepts as the "frozen zoo," is that people might begin to think that all the problems of endangered animals can be solved in the zoo. They might get the idea that even if an animal actually becomes extinct, somehow, some way, it can be brought back in the future through the use of frozen embryos or some other wonderful technique.

It isn't going to happen that way. If the history of the various captive breeding programs teach anything, it is that this is a difficult and expensive process which does not always work.

It is worth repeating: The best and most permanent way of preserving species of animals is to preserve the environment. For all the success some captive breeding programs have had in the past, and for all the success many more may have in the future, they are still a stop-gap measure. They are not so much a sign of our success in breeding animals in zoos, but of our failure to be able to keep them alive in nature.

AZA Species Survival Plans

MAMMALS

Addax
African wild dog
Arabian oryx
Asian small-clawed otter
Asian wild horse
Barasingha
Black-footed ferret
Black lemur
Black rhinoceros
Bonobo (pygmy chimpanzee)
Chacoan peccary
Cheetah
Chimpanzee
Clouded leopard
Cotton-top tamarin
Drill
Elephant (African, Asian)
Gaur
Giant panda
Gibbon (siamang, white-
cheeked, white-handed)
Goeldi's monkey (callimico)
Golden lion tamarin
Greater one-horned Asian
rhinoceros
Grevy's zebra
Lion-tailed macaque
Lowland gorilla
Maned wolf
Mexican gray wolf
Okapi
Orangutan
Pygmy hippopotamus
Red panda
Red wolf
Rodrigues' fruit bat
Ruffed lemur
Snow leopard
Spectacled bear
Sumatran rhinoceros
Tiger
Tree kangaroo (Doria's,

Goodfellow's, grizzled,
Matschiei's)
White rhinoceros

BIRDS

Bali mynah
Cinereous vulture
Condor (Andean, California)
Crane (hooded, red-crowned,
wattled, white-naped)
Guam rail
Humboldt penguin
Micronesian kingfisher
Pink pigeon
St. Vincent parrot
Thick-billed parrot

REPTILES AND AMPHIBIANS

Aruba island rattlesnake
Chinese alligator
Duméril's ground boa
Mona/Virgin Islands boa
Puerto Rican crested toad
Radiated tortoise

FISH

Haplochromine cichlids

INVERTEBRATES

Partula snail

BIBLIOGRAPHY

BOOKS

Brons, Bill. *A World of Animals.* New York: Harry N. Abrams, 1983.

Crandall, Lee S. *The Management of Wild Mammals in Captivity.* Chicago: University of Chicago Press, 1964.

DeBlieu, Jan. *Meant to Be Wild.* Golden, CO: Fulcrum Publishing, 1991.

Embery, Joan. *My Wild World.* New York: Delacorte, 1980.

Gold, Don. *Zoo.* Chicago: Contemporary Books, 1988.

Hannah, Jack. *Monkeys on the Interstate.* New York: Doubleday, 1989.

Hoage, R. J. *Animal Extinctions: What Everyone Should Know.* Washington, D.C.: Smithsonian Institution Press, 1985.

Hoagland, Edward. *Red Wolves and Black Bears.* New York: Random House, 1976.

Mullan, Bob, and Garry Marvin. *Zoo Culture.* London: Weidenfeld & Nicolson, 1987.

Schaller, George B. *The Last Panda.* Chicago: University of Chicago Press, 1993.

Sedgwick, John. *The Peaceable Kingdom.* New York: William Morrow, 1988.

Wiesse, Robert J., Beth Zebrowski, Leanne Willbanks, Michael Hutchins, and Karen Allen. *Species Survival Plans*. Bethesda, MD: AAZPA, 1992.

PERIODICALS

Banks, Vic. "The Red Wolf Gets a Second Chance to Live by Its Wits." *Smithsonian*, March 1988.

Burnham, Laurie. "Off and Running: The Cheetah Master Plan." *Scientific American*, February 1988.

Carpenter, Betsy. "Back from the Abyss." *U.S. News & World Report*, 14 October 1991.

DeBlieu, Jan. "Could the Red Wolf Be a Mutt?" *The New York Times* Magazine, 14 June 1992.

———."Remodeling the Condor." *The New York Times* Magazine, 17 November 1991.

Di Silvestro, Roger. "Saga of AC-9, the Last Free Condor." *Audubon*, July 1987.

Ezzell, Carol. "Conserving a Coyote in Wolf's Clothing?" *Science News*, 15 June 1991.

Gilbert, Bil. "This Scarface Is a Real Animal." *Sports Illustrated*, 8 April 1991.

Luoma, Jon R., "Born to Be Wild." *Audubon*, January/February 1992.

O'Brien, Stephen J., David E. Wildt, and Mitchell Bush. "The Cheetah in Genetic Peril." *Scientific American*, May 1986.

Oliwenstein, Lori. "Free as a Bird." *Discovery*, January 1993.

Park, Edwards. "Around the Mall and Beyond" (column). *Smithsonian*, October 1990.

Pennisi, Elizabeth. "Cheetah Countdown: Does Inbreeding—or Zoo Life—Hinder This Feline's Fecundity?" *Science News*, 25 September 1993.

Radatsky, Peter. "Back to Nature." *Discover*, July 1993.

Robarts, Leslie. "Beyond Noah's Ark: What Do We Need to Know?" *Science*, December 1988.

Roema, John. "El Condor Passé: Is It Time to Write Off California's Big Bird?" *California*, May 1988.

Sharpe, Patricia. "The Wolf Experiment." *Texas Monthly,* September 1989.

Steinhart, Peter. "In the Blood of Cheetahs." *Audubon,* March/April 1992.

Weinberg, David. "Decline and Fall of the Black-Footed Ferret." *Natural History,* February 1986.

Williams, Martin. "Conservation Hotline: Signs of Change in China." *Wildlife Conservation,* January/February 1994.

Willworth, James. "Can They Go Home Again?" *Time,* 27 January 1992.

INDEX

Page entries in italics indicate illustrations in the text.

117